Cabin of the Great Western in a Storm.

CURRENT AMERICAN NOTES

BY

"BUZ!"

CHAPTER I.

THE DEPARTURE FROM ENGLAND.

THERE are few positions more fraught with pleasing, and, at the same time, more powerful feelings than a departure from the land of our birth. "Every kind of parting hath its sting," and there is, whether under circumstances of the most dire necessity, or those which spring only from the love of adventure or change, an agony in the word "farewell." For myself I must confess, that I am a Cockney, and, more than that, I am proud of that denomination. My peregrinations had heretofore been confined to land jaunts to the green hill of Richmond, or the more dangerous task of going to "Woolwich by water," and it was not without vast consideration, and "screwing my courage to the sticking point," that I at length determined on crossing the wide Atlantic. I have said I am a Cockney, and that I am proud of it, and I have good and sufficient authority to warrant my assumption. Shade of the immortal Whittington; and thou less known, though no less hallowed in the heart of those who have been fortunate enough to read thy "strange eventful history," Haldebert Watts, the London apprentice—could I but make up in future story, the cockney trio I should die content!

My visit to America, gentle reader, was undertaken from no selfish motive; I had heard and read the various garbled accounts given by interested adventurers of that "land of the brave, and home of the free," and therefore, determined, for the satisfaction of my fellow-countrymen, to sacrifice my time and comforts to elucidate the truth. I have made me a fame—I occupy a niche in the temple of English literature—I shall, as the immortal Byron says, " live in my land's language ;" and it is no elongation of the imagination to say, that the name of " Charles Stretch, Esq.," will go down to fame with those of the illustrious past !

It was, to use a theatrical phrase, with feelings of a serio-comic nature that I entered the state-room of the Great Western steam-ship, bound to New York, it was in the month of January, eighteen hundred and forty-two. " And is this," I said, " the state-room of which my friend Benson, who had kindly arranged all matters for my voyage, spoke in terms of rapturous delight ?" I looked around me ; yes, I was not mistaken ; for, pinned on a very flat quilt, over a very thin mat-trass, spread like the butter on the piece of bread which some spoilt child had neglected for breakfast, and placed on a high shelf to be eaten for his dinner, was a manuscript, announcing that this state-room had been expressly engaged for " Charles Stretch, Esq., and lady." It's pleasant, they say, to read your name in print, but I confess, at that moment, that simple manuscript announcement went to my heart, " Charles Stretch, Esq., and lady." There was something in its simplicity that Sterne would have lovingly descanted on. That mighty ship, with her engines, her paddles, and her machinery—her white sails and her black stokers—the three thousand miles of green water which she would traverse—the storms she might encounter, and there would be in that state-room " Charles Stretch, Esq., and lady." Previously to visiting the vessel, my wife and I had often talked over the probable size of the " state-room." Was it as spacious as our front drawing-room in Portman-square, or as commodious, even, as our back drawing-room ?—was it as large, even, as our dining room, or my library, or her boudoir ? Was it, even, in its dimensions, to be compared to her lady's-maid's apartment, or my gentleman's sleeping room ? Alas ! for the vanity of all human speculations ! This state apartment, when seen, instead of bearing comparison with front or back drawing-rooms, dining room, library, boudoir, lady's-maid's apartment, or dormitory of gentleman's gentleman dwindled down to the dimensions of the back garret of a penny-a-liner.

I shall not attempt to narrate the various petty disappointments and annoyances I met with on viewing the internal arrangements. The vivid descriptions given by the proprietors on paper ill accord with the appearance of the vessel when in actual service. There is as much difference between a vessel in the docks, with her trim carpet and silken curtains, and the same ship under weigh with her creaking cordage, sloppy floors, and compound of villanous smells, as between the *hanging* wood described by the auctioneer as ornamenting the mansion he was puffing for sale, and the identical gibbet which the credulous buyer found adorning the vicinity of his purchase. But the Captain has just stept on board—a fine, bluff, weather-beaten fellow, looking the very picture of confidence and courage, and, indeed, a man whose very features almost insure you from the remotest chance of your destiny, whilst under his care, inclining to drowning.

The last thing waited for has arrived—'tis the mail bags; these are dragged in and thrown anywhere; all is bustle and confusion. "Good byes, and God bless-yous!" resound, mingled with a few other imprecations of a contrary nature. At length the anchor is heaved up, three cheers are given, 'midst smoke, smother, and noise; first an explosion, like an enormous sneeze, and then the floating leviathan groans into life—its mighty wheels throw the salt spray high in air, and away it goes like a thing of life through the foaming waters.

We dined, the first day on board, eighty-six strong. The wind blew freshly and we did not muster our full force; six gentlemen and two ladies not having finished bringing up their breakfasts before the dinner bell rang. One lady made a precipitate retreat from the table on being helped to a very bilious-looking slice of boiled mutton with caper sauce. As evening approached, the perpetual tramp of boot-heels on the decks gave way to a heavy silence, and soon all the passengers were stowed away below, excepting a very few stragglers like myself, who, perhaps, were half afraid to go there. This is the striking time on shipboard. The gloom through which the vessel holds its certain course—the rushing waters heard, but dimly seen, and the white foaming track that follows in her course; the helmsman at the wheel, with the illuminated card before him—the melancholy sighing of the wind through block and chain—the gleaming light from every crevice, nook, and tiny pane of glass about the deck—all these things act upon the imagination, and assume the form and shape of well-remembered scenes.

Being forced at length, by the cold, below, I found things not so comfortable as I expected. I had some difficulty in walking the deck and I now found everything sloped upwards. I left the door of, my state room open; when I turned to shut it the handle eluded my grasp, and the door appeared to have run up to the ceiling; and now strange noises disturbed the more timid; the ship creaked and groaned; and then there was a crackling noise like a bundle of twigs over a fire. There was no alternative but bed and brandy-and-water; but the brandy-and-water tasted like bilge water, and the biscuits I attempted to eat, like cheese rind.

On the third morning things got much worse. When I awoke I looked for my clothes; everything was jumping about like lively turtle. The water jug appeared alive, and my shoes were floating. The door appeared to be in the floor, and a looking-glass, which had been nailed against the wall, fixed in the ceiling; in fact, the whole room was standing on its head. I made my way with some difficulty up the staircase to the companion way—heaven! what a sight met my eyes. I had heard of the great green waters, and there they stood on one side of the vessel like a monstrous wall, that seemed to threaten every instant to fall and overwhelm us.

"What do you call this, Captain?" said I.

"Rather a heavy sea," he replied, "and a head wind."

I shall never forget the labouring of the ship on the troubled sea through the following night. Now she was flung on her side in the waves, with her masts dipping into them, and then, springing up again. She rolled over on the other side, until a heavy sea struck her with the noise of thunder and hurled her back. Then she stopped, staggered, and shivered as though stunned, and then, with a violent throbbing, darted onward like a monster goaded into madness, to be beaten down and battered, and crushed, and leaped on by the angry sea. The thunder, lightning, hail, and rain, and wind, are all fiercely contending together. The planks groan, and the ocean has a howling voice, appalling, wild, and horrible.

Half dead with sickness, I was sitting at the table in the saloon, for I could not sleep. Opposite to me was a regular Yankee, who had forced his acquaintance upon me on first coming aboard. Amidst all the horrors of the night the rain came down in torrents. The Yankee was perfectly cool and composed, and was imbibing "considerable," as he said, " of brandy-and-water."

" Pretty saft night this," said he, " good for the yearth."

" I don't know what it may be for the earth," I replied, " but its bad enough at sea."

" Aye," answered he, " just such a night as this when the President went down, I guess."

This was too much to bear. I staggered from my seat as well as I could, and sought the state room to cheer my wife, and gaze on her, perhaps, for the last time.

The following morning the wind lulled and the storm abated; but still the rolling of the vessel was tremendous. I was regularly as a married man, and, having my wife with me, installed in the ladies' cabin. Early in the day we shipped a heavy sea—the last that broke over us: but it appeared that we were fated to remember it as such. It forced our cabin door open, and came rushing in, to the great alarm of its inmates. There were two ladies in the cabin, besides my wife and her maid. They were dreadfully alarmed. I thought of the general remedy for sea-sickness and fear, and, with some difficulty, procured a glass of brandy-and-water from the steward, and tried to administer it to them. This I found a difficult task. The vessel pitched so much that they could not stand up. When I tried to get to them on one side, they all suddenly rolled to the other; and when I staggered to that end, the ship gave a lurch, and they all rolled back again. At length, in making a desperate effort, I fell forward myself, and the captain opening the door to inquire how we all were at the time, I dashed the brandy-and-water full into his face. Two hours after this, I managed to get upon deck. The ocean and sky appeared of the same dull, leaden, uniform colour; the sea still rolled heavily; and, as the wave formed a long line of dark wall, I perceived the heads of several large monsters of the deep protruding out of it : they were grampuses, who were enjoying themselves on the surface of the water, and gambolling about, as if rejoicing at the subsiding storm. They looked like the dark guards of the ocean, stretching out their long and gloomy line of defence. The weather still continued bad, and confined us a great deal to our cabin; but we managed to wile away the time by reading, and a quiet game at whist, at which sometimes the Captain joined us. It was amusing to see the cool, easy way in which he left the cabin, when called to go upon deck, when he turned up the collar of his dreadnought coat, put on his nor-wester, and stepped out into the storm and darkness, as carelessly and merrily as if he was going to a wedding.

There was no dearth of news and gossip on board: every one wondered how the pale young man in black could afford to play so high at loo in the saloon; and others wondered who the young couple could be who kept so much aloof from the rest of the passengers. Amongst the number in the cabin was a young Englishman, who had evidently come out on some speculation; but what it was no one could guess. At length, one morning, being on deck, I was placed in such a situation that I could, without being seen, overhear a conversation between him and the Yankee previously mentioned.

" Well," said the Yankee, " but this beats cock-fighting! And so you've come out to trade in Ingens ?"

" Not exactly," replied the Cockney, " to say trade; but I want to get some four or five that can shoot well, and do all sorts of tricks, like those they had at the Cobourg theatre some years back."

" Well, then," said the Yankee, " I guess you'd better try to catch some."

" Catch 'em !" cried the Cockney, with some astonishment; " but how ? Are there any in the woods near New York ?"

" 'Bundance—'bundance," answered the Yankee, " and tigers on the pantiles of the houses just out of town. It's a mortal place for wild animals."

" You don't say so ?" replied the Cockney. " But are the Indians very difficult to catch ?"

" The easiest thing in the world," said the Yankee. " They all wear one long bit of hair, that hangs right away from the crown of their heads; just get a grip at that, then hold on like grim death to a dead nigger, and you have 'em slick as grease !"

" Well, now, that's what I call sharp," answered the Cockney.

" Sharp ! I guess it is !" rejoined the Yankee. " My father was one of the sharpest men in all Connecticut. What do you think he did one day, stranger ?"

" I can't guess, I'm sure," replied the Cockney.

" No; you English never guess," said the Yankee, " you think. Well, father once sharpened a scythe so slick, that when he hung it up in the sun the shadow cut a man's leg off !"

Just then the bell rang for dinner, and I was deprived of the chance of being further edified in the art of catching Ingens or sharpening scythes.

In a few days the weather cleared up, and after running with a favourable breeze, we made Sandy Hook, passed Staten Island, and were safely landed at the Battery at New York.

New York is a fine city; it is considered by most foreigners to be the capital of the State, but it is not so—the capital being Albany, on the Hudson River. There are many bye streets, almost as neutral in clean colours, and positive in dirty ones, as bye streets in London; and there is one quarter, commonly called the Five Points, which, in respect of filth and wretchedness, may be safely backed against Seven Dials, or any other part of famed St. Giles.

The great promenade and thoroughfare, as most people know, is Broadway, a wide and bustling street, which, from the Battery Gardens to its opposite termination in a country road, may be four miles long. Now let us forth from our tavern, the inimitable Astor House, and mingle in the throng. No stint of omnibuses here—half-a-dozen have gone by in as many minutes; plenty of hackney cabs and coaches, tod-gigs, phaetons, large wheeled tilburies and private carriages, rather of a clumsy make, and not very different from the public vehicles, but built for the heavy roads beyond the city pavements. Negro coachmen and white, in straw hats, black hats, white hats, glazed caps, fur caps; in coats of drab, black, brown, green, blue, nankeen, striped jean, and linen; and there, in that one instance (look while it passes, or it will be too late), in suit of livery.

This narrow thoroughfare; baking and blistering in the sun, is Wall-street—the Stock Exchange and Lombard-street of New York. Many a rapid fortune has been made in this street, and many a no less rapid ruin.

What is this dismal fronted pile of bastard Egyptian, like an enchanter's palace in a melo-drama? A famous prison, called the Tombs. Shall we go in?

So—a long, narrow building, stove-heated, as usual, with four galleries, one above another, going round it, and communicating by stairs. Between the two sides of each gallery, and in its centre, a bridge for the greater convenience of crossing. On each of these bridges sits a man dozing or reading, or talking to his idle companion; on each tier are two opposite rows of small iron doors. They look like furnace-doors, but are cold and black, as though the fires within had all gone out.

A man with keys appears, to show us round—a good looking fellow, and in his way civil and obliging.

" Are these black doors cells?"

" Yes."

" Are they all full?"

" Well, they're pretty nigh full, and that's a fact, and no two ways about it."

" Those at the bottom are unwholesome, surely?"

" Why, we *do* only put coloured people in 'em—that's the truth."

" When do the prisoners take exercise?"

" Well, they do without it pretty much."

" Do they never walk in the yard?"

" Considerable seldom."

" Sometimes, I suppose ?"

" Well, its rare they do. They keep pretty bright without."

" Will you open one of the doors ?"

" All, if you like."

The fastenings jar and rattle, and one of the doors turns slowly on its hinges. Let us look in. A small, bare cell, into which the light enters through a high chink in the wall. There is a rude means of washing, a table, and a bedstead.

Here is seated a man who has been condemned to seven years' solitary confinement for robbery. He was a shoemaker, and was allowed to work at his trade. He was a most ingenious mechanic, and had, to wile away his time, made a clock with such rude materials as he could collect in his prison. He showed it us with much pride, and asked us for the exact time, and was highly gratified to find that his clock was tolerably correct. He appeared cheerful and contented ; he had notched on a stick the months, weeks, and days of his captivity, four years of which he had endured. When questioned as to his feelings, the tear stood in his eye as he spoke of his wife. Where was she—did she feel an interest in his fate—or had she forgotten him ? After speaking a few minutes he turned away, and seemed to wish we would terminate our visit, and set heartily and steadily to his work.

We left the cell, by no means envying him his feelings.

" He's a spry workman," said the jailor, " and made me these shoes."

Another door is opened. Here a German was confined for life, for an attempted murder. His little cell he had painted over in the most exquisite style ; he was an artist of great skill. The little yard adjoining he had turned into a garden ; there was not a speck of dirt or disorder in the room, everything was in order, and he appeared to have a nervous pleasure in picking up the smallest pebbles, or in renovating the slightest injury given by time or chance to his work in the room. His countenance was ghastly in the extreme ; hope appeared to have fled for ever from his desolate heart, and he looked as one to whom all things had ceased to be. We left him with an aching heart and sought another. Here was a young, fair girl, who, with others, had been concerned in an extensive robbery of their employers. She looked calm, pensive—but not unhappy. When questioned as to her feelings, she replied—

" I am happy, excepting—"

" Excepting what ?" I asked.

" That my friends are not with me ; 'tis so hard to have no one to talk to."

Poor thing ! I pitied her, indeed. Hers was a misfortune which all my fair friends can well appreciate. No one to talk to—why there is madness in the very thought.

I observed that confinement does not, however, have so brutalizing an effect upon the female sex as upon men ; there was a placidity and calmness about this young girl that many a busy dame might envy, and it has been found to effectually cure them, on their enlargement, from any inclination for a repetition of crime.

But now we are in the cell of one convicted of a most atrocious murder—a murder the most revolting, as his own child was the hapless victim. He was described as having been a ruffian of the lowest caste debauched and drunken in the extreme; we were prepared to see a man bearing on his brow an index of his mind—to read there the legible characters of crime—what was our surprise to find, seated calmly on his bed, a pale-faced man, with an intellectual head, and a cast of features which would anywhere have been pronounced decidedly interesting. His employment was equally extraordinary, he had tamed a canary bird, and it was hopping on his hand, feeding from his mouth, and expressing, by various little endearments, its confidence in its blood-stained master.

"Has this man any hopes of ever seeing the outside of his prison, think you?" said I to the gaoler.

"Guess he has," replied he.

"How so—is he not confined for life?"

"Oh, certainly."

"On what, then, are his hopes founded?"

"Perhaps in friends."

"Can such a man have friends?

"Everybody's got somebody that feels for him. Then, perhaps, he may have interest in Congress."

This was enough—I asked no more. The bare idea of a murderer in the prison of the Tombs having interest in Congress was too ridiculous!

"Is not your employment here very irksome?" said I to the gaoler.

"Not at all," he replied; "besides, I have my time out."

I was anxious to know what the bent of his inclinations was as regarded amusement, and asked him how he generally employed his time.

"I go to the playhouse whenever I can get a chance," said he. "But I don't care much to go now: they play nothing but melodramas. Now, I like the genuine thing. Give me Shakspere, or the opera. As for all the rubbish about murders and prisons, I see enough of that every day. And, besides, they never do it natural: never saw a gaoler well played in my life; and as for the way they let the prisoners get out and escape—why, a baby could see through all that."

I could not but commend his penetration. There is one more cell: it is opened.

"Is not this the cell that Mina, the poisoner, was confined in previous to his execution?"

"It is so."

We had already seen enough of this place of horrors, and were glad to escape into the open air. When seated over our wine, I asked my friend, a lawyer of great eminence, if there was anything very extraordinary about the person he had mentioned.

"Yes," he replied; "and I will with pleasure relate his history. Few men had so strange and eventful a career as

"THEODORE MINA!"

CHAPTER II.

"How that pale lip will curl and quiver,
Then fix once more—and that for ever."

BYRON.

"If ever evil angel bore
The form of mortal, such he wore."

Ibid.

MINA, THE POISONER.

IT was a bright autumnal evening, and the sun's last rays shed a parting gleam over the wild scenery of the Highlands, as the Majestic, one of the noblest of the steam craft that navigate the Hudson, cleft her way rapidly through the calm waters on her passage from Albany to New York..

The deck, fore and aft, was crowded with passengers. A band of musicians played from time to time several of Mozart's and Rossini's celebrated overtures; whilst music breathed, champagne exploded; charming mouths dropped words of wit and mirth; groups of sylphs and syrens reclaimed the wandering curl; whilst worshippers, with collars bent to the precise angle-cravats, tied in the approved knot, with glossy boots, curled heads, crooked elbows, and audacious whiskers, whispered soft nonsense into willing ears.

Such were the majority of the parties occupying the more aristocratical portion of the vessel, whilst the forecastle, thronged with a more motley group, was equally rife with bustle and excitement. Amidst the smoke of cigars, allowable only in this part of the vessel, might be perceived a group of New York dandies, standing at the extreme edge of the line to shew their more plebeian associates that the gratification of their fumatory enjoyments was the sole cause that brought them into so disgusting a proximity.

At short intervals cider and brandy were loudly called for, and under their combined influence a storekeeper, from Chatham-street, might be seen in one corner making a most injudicious "swop" in the article of

watches, with a knowing " Down Easter," whilst a missionary agent'
and a member of the Temperance Society, were forcing their tracts into
the hands of a drunken party engaged in the interesting game of
" blind hookey."

Amidst, but evidently not belonging to any of the numerous grades
assembled in this part of the Majestic, stood, leaning by the vessel's
side, a man whose appearance and bearing would have rendered him,
under any circumstances, an object of attention.

He was above the common height, with a frame, the very perfection
at once of strength and agility. His face, despite a peculiar expression,
might have been pronounced superlatively handsome. His dark shining
locks, though cut much too close for the prevailing fashion, curled
closely round a finely proportioned head, and his splendidly marked
moustache, although evidently but of a few days growth, gave a striking
expression to a mouth, which, but for this adornment, might have been
considered almost feminine. His dress was decidedly shabby, but the
well cut and highly embroidered military frock, the high-heeled boots,
with the spur-holes, although cracked and cobbled, with linen of dazzling whiteness, evidently told of better and of brighter fortunes. His
features were decidedly Spanish, although in the various attempts of
conversation forced upon him, it was observed he spoke English fluently |
The dark olive complexion had given way to a more pallid and almost
sickly hue, although the bright eye, moist lip, and dazzling teeth
denied the presence of bodily disease. He continued to maintain the
position he had first assumed on coming on board the vessel, and gazed
around apparently abstracted and unmoved, although many a group
of fair girls passed the line interdicted by fashion, on some pretext, to
gaze on the handsome stranger, and more than one bright eye blended
pity with its ardent glance of admiration.

Amongst the numbers comprising the passengers of the Majestic,
was a female fast approaching the meridian of life, but still retaining the
remains of surpassing beauty. She was married, and the mother of five
children, two of whom were with her, returning to her place of residence, a village on the banks of the Hudson, from a visit to a relative
in Albany. She had observed with some attention the stranger
previously described, on entering the boat at Albany. No opportunity
of communication had occurred; but, during the day, the dark eye of the
unknown had frequently encountered the wild and impassioned gaze of
this usually sedate and quiet matron.

A moment will suffice to decide the fate of man or woman, and during
that brief journey, the hitherto blameless wife and mother sealed her
doom of misery and guilt in the unhallowed glance exchanged between
herself and the *felon* Mina. It might have had its origin in pity, or in
blameless admiration; but, "rebellious hell at times will mutine in a
matron's bones." The incipient vice, the dormant passion, may be
kindled by the slightest spark, and the virtue of years yield on the
instant to the dark internal whisperings of the tempter.

Of the early history of Theodore Mina, an individual who, for a brief period, occupied a great portion of public attention, but little is known. He had assumed the name, and claimed near consanguinity to the celebrated Spanish patriot; he had, evidently, though not five-and-twenty, mixed in superior and polished society, he spoke most of the European languages, was highly accomplished; and these circumstances, blended with an excessively prepossessing exterior, and the most insinuating manners, rendered him, perhaps, one of the most dangerous adventurers that ever preyed upon the credulity of his fellows.

From his confessions, made previous to his death, he acknowledged having left the Havannah from a fear of punishment for the murder of a Portuguese merchant in the open day in a coffee house, but of which he always spoke in terms of extreme levity; and if courage may be tested by coolness and unflinching resolution up to the latest period of existence. no one had a greater claim to that quality than Theodore Mina.

At the period of our story he had just been liberated from the States prison of Buffalo, where he had endured, with the same philosophic calmness that marked his after conduct, all the misery and degradation of a year's solitary confinement. His head had been, agreeably to custom, half shaved, which accounted for the close crop of hair previously described, and the moustache was but the growth of the two days following his liberation, when his convict dress had been replaced by his own clothes, and money given him to bear him from the States. Such was the first public appearance of Mina on the stage of American life—his previous committal to the jail of Buffalo having taken place within a few days of his first arrival in the States.

It was nearly dark when the steam boat arrived at " Ploughkeepsie," and the boat was lowered for the purpose of conveying such of the passengers as were anxious to land at the village, amongst whom was the female before mentioned and her children. The boat was on the point of leaving, when Mina, who had hitherto appeared entirely unconcerned, presented himself as a passenger, took his place at the opposite extremity to which she was seated, and on [the boat reaching its destination, without having exchanged a word with any person, left it, and walked leisurely towards a small tavern near the water's edge.

A car (or waggon as it is called in America), under the care of a servant, awaited the arrival of the female and her children, in which, after some luggage had been placed, they entered, and were soon out of the sight of our adventurer.

Previously to entering the public-house, Mina exchanged some words with a servant of the establishment, who had been assisting to place the luggage into the waggon. He now passed into the public room, and called for refreshment. His appearance produced some attention from the landlord (who, like all his craft, was both curious and communicative), the dress of the adventurer, as observed by the dim twilight, not being such as to prejudice him against its wearer.

" How far is it to the residence of Mr. Chapman ?" inquired Mina.

" I guess you know him then ?" replied the landlord, asking instead of answering a question, after the approved fashion of transatlantic manners.

"Slightly," said the adventurer.

"I calculate, then, you're not awful intimate with his *wife*, 'cause she came in the same boat with you," resumed he of the spigot, glancing his eye rather suspiciously over the person of his companion.

"No," said Mina, nowise taken aback.

"I have some business with Mr. Chapman; and I suppose I shall find him at home?"

"Why, for the matter of that," continued the landlord, "I don't think he's likely to be out, seeing that he's kept his bed these three months."

"Indeed!" resumed Mina, "I'm sorry to hear it. It is not far, I know, from here, and I dare say I shall find my way."

"Oh, no," said mine host; "just keep due north up the road, about a mile, and you'll find the place. Its a large white house, a few yards back, on the left. You'll know it by two large beech trees before the door. Take care of yourself, though; he keeps two uncommon powerful cross-grained dogs—and they aint particular noways."

"Good night," said Mina, and he left the house. The landlord watched him until nearly out of sight.

"Don't half like that chap," said he to his wife; "got an uncommon foreign look about him: but there's plenty of people about Chapman's place; and I know the dogs are loose by this time; and I'll back black Wolf alone against any 'two-legged creetur:'" and, lighting a cigar, he wended his way into the parlour, to give his company (such as it was) to his guests.

The residence of Mr. Chapman, a substantial and wealthy farmer, was a large commodious house, standing on a rising ground a short distance from the high road. Convenient offices surrounded it, and its approach was by a large gate, which led into a lawn and garden before the door.

The proprietor of the premises had been confined some time by a violent attack of fever and ague, which, although attended by no immediate danger, had produced so great a prostration of strength, as to render him unable to leave his chamber.

Lights were burning in the large parlour, or common sitting-room, and Mrs. Chapman, the female alluded to in the earlier part of our story, was seated with her eldest son and daughter at supper. Her son was about fifteen years of age, and her daughter about two years younger. The other children were in bed, the youngest being but four years of age, and the eldest eight. A fever spot was on her cheek, and her eye was wild and unsettled. The servant had placed chamber lights upon the table, and her daughter was in the act of retiring, when the outer bell rung with some degree of violence, and the loud baying of the dogs proclaimed the approach of a stranger. A man-servant answered the door, and returned, saying a stranger wished to speak with his mistress. Mina had by this time entered the garden, and advanced towards the door, which the servants had left unopened. Mrs. Chapman arose, passed out into the portico, and saw, standing uncovered, full in the pale moonlight, the object of her interest and admiration on board the steam-boat. What passed between them in that brief interview is unknown—enough, that in a few minutes the adventurer was seated at the table. The supper was renewed, a bed-room was prepared for him, and it was a late hour before the unhappy wife sought the couch of her invalid husband.

Weeks passed away, and still found the felon adventurer domesticated beneath the farmer's hospitable roof. His dress became improved, he rode a good horse, was well provided with money, and, as well mounted and equipped, he passed the "Indian King," at the end of the village, Jacob Peabody, the landlord, was heard to say, "that, despite his whiskers and yellow face, he was certainly an uncommon *spry-looking* chap."

The health of Mr. Chapman was by this time considerably improved; and as he had no jealous fears as regarded his wife's intimacy with a man young enough to be her son, his kindness and hospitality towards Mina remained undiminished. With the increasing convalescence of her husband, the air and manner of the guilty wife became moody and abstracted. Did she regret his recovery, or fear in his renewed health and spirits a more close observation of her conduct? Alas! no. A more fearful reason lurked in that tone of listlessness and discontent. She feared that he would live to mar her guilty joys. One absorbing passion alone occupied her thoughts, and his presence seemed a dark cloud to its brightness—a wall of adamant to its full completion!

It was a dark night at the latter end of December. The wind moaned dismally without, and the wild roar of the swollen river mingled with the raging blast : all had retired to rest save Mina and his matron mistress. They were seated opposite each other in the large old parlour. The long wicks on the candles proved the abstraction of both ; he was leaning with his head upon the table as if half asleep.

"You will leave me then, Theodore," said she, raising and placing her arm around his neck; " I know this dull place does not suit you, and I am but a sorry companion."

" Not so," replied Mina ; " but I cannot consent longer to share only in that I love so well," and he raised his dark eyes to her face.

She kissed his lips and forehead.

" What shall I do ?" she cried wildly, " all would I barter for your love."

Mina drew her towards him, and whispered close into her ear. So breathed the tempter into that of our first mother in the dream that presaged her fall. She spoke not—started not—replied not ; but threw herself on the neck of her destroyer and wept.

Mina took from his pocket-book a small paper packet.

" Put one of these," said he, with fiendish calmness, " into his cup at breakfast ; repeat it for some few mornings in succession ; it will tell no tales.   It is *not* poison," said he, emphatically, "it will produce ease and sleep for him," and, he continued in a deep whisper, " and for you and for one—"

—" At all risk—at all peril," said the wretched wife, and they parted with mutual protestations of endearment.

In a few days the health of Mr. Chapman was observed visibly to decline.   He had a great dislike to medical advice ; and his wife, for reasons best known to herself, encouraged his aversion.   Mina had studied medicine, and took upon himself the office of family physician.

The children were too young to interfere, had they been so inclined ; and his few friends were, under various pretences, denied to him.   Day by day he continued to sink, until nature appeared exhausted ; and one morning his death was announced to the domestics of the family and his neighbours, as having taken place suddenly in the night.

Great grief was manifested by his widow, to whom the whole of his property had been left.   Although remarks had been made in the little community of Poughkeepsie, respecting the foreign inmate of Burley farm, as yet, no suspicion was entertained of the truth.

The funeral was attended by the principal inhabitants ; and Mina, in solemn black, undertook for his widow the direction of her late husband's affairs.

Soon after the death of Mr. Chapman, the elder children were placed at school, and the widow, with the younger ones and Mina, removed to the neighbourhood of Utica.   There they in a short time afterwards proclaimed their marriage, and a general feeling of indignation was aroused against the lost and abandoned pair.

Mina, who had obtained his wish in the possession of a great portion of the property of his victim, now treated his guilty partner with neglect. The usual bickerings and recriminations followed, and one morning, after a quarrel of unusual violence, he left her and set off for the South.

Mrs. Chapman returned to Poughkeepsie, and here a new misery awaited her.   Scandal had been very busy in her absence.   One of the servants had reported that on the night Mr. Chapman died, as it was said, without a groan or struggle, he heard loud shrieks and convulsive moans proceeding evidently from the chamber of his master.   Suspicion was aroused, curiosity awakened, and in the course of inquiry many circumstances were elicited which threw, at least, strong presumption of guilt on Mina and herself.

At length the authorities were applied to by some relatives of the deceased ; the body was exhumed and opened, and, from the opinion generally given, no doubt remained that the unfortunate man had been *poisoned!*

Mrs. Chapman was taken into custody, and a warrant issued for the apprehension of Mina, who at that precise moment was about to honour with his hand and fortune one of the richest heiresses and most beautiful girls in the city of Baltimore, but who fortunately escaped such destiny by the arrest of her lover on his return from a scene of warm and impassioned courtship.

Mina was tried for the murder, when, finding evidence being brought forward likely to criminate his paramour, with a feeling worthy of a better cause, he confessed the crime for which he was arraigned, and protested to the last moment the innocence of his companion.

He met his fate by the hands of the executioner, with all that pride and firmness which had distinguished his life. Dressed with studious elegance, and his dark locks perfumed and arranged with the minutest care (for which purpose he had two hair-dressers in attendance

on the morning of execution), many a cheek was blanched, and many a bright eye dimmed with tears, as the form of the " handsome Mina" swung darkly in the morning breeze.

Such was the fate of Theodore Mina, but to show how strangely society is constituted in this country, although there was not the slightest doubt in most persons' minds that Mrs. Chapman, was, if not the instigator, the willing and positive agent in the murder; she was a few years since positively moving in respectable society, and for some time kept a school at Utica. Whether she was calculated to bring up the female mind in the paths of virtue, and " teach the young idea how to shoot," is best known to those who chose to trust their children to her care ; but those parties who, when spoken to upon the subject, justified their own conduct in patronising her, by saying, " that at any rate whatever might have been her conduct as regarded the late unfortunate affair, everybody must allow she was an uncommon smart woman !"

———————

CHAPTER III.

" This is Alsatia, sir."

SCOTT.

" A fig for St. Denis of France,
    He's a trumpery fellow to brag on ;
A fig for St. George and his lance,
    Which spitted a heathenish dragon.
And the saints of the Welchman and Scot
    Are a couple of pitiful pipers ;
Both of whom may just travel to pot,
    Compared with the patron of swipers,
        St. Patrick of Ireland, my dear."

MAGINN.

'TIS bright morning and we will again stroll down the Broadway. Look at those two labourers dressed decently in their holiday clothes ; one is trying to spell some hard name on a crumpled paper he carries in his hand, whilst the other peers curiously about for it on all the doors and windows.

Patlanders both ; look at their long-tailed blue coats, their drab trowsers, which they wear with that uneasy air all working men feel out of their ordinary dresses, and yet this great Republic would scarcely be kept going without them ; for the Americans, like the Jews, never work : 'tis the poor Irish—who are in reality transported serfs, to dig a soil they have no part or parcel in—'tis they who make canals and roads, and execute the great lines of internal improvement. Let's go down and help them to find out the direction they are so bothered about ; but now two more have joined them—four beautiful specimens they are of " the first gem of the ocean."

"What a pity," said one of them, "that we left Teague behind, for he could read like a book."

But how came Teague to be left behind? It appears they were all from sweet Kilkenny, boon companions and sworn brothers; had made up their minds to leave the " old sod," and wend their way to Ameriky. They were five in number : two Paddies, one Murphy, one Dennis, and one Teague. It so happened that the vessel that they were to go in could only take four of them. At length honest Teague exclaimed, " Arrah! I have it. We'll cast losts to see who shall remain." But one of the Paddies swore it was not jonteel to do that thing. "You know, Teague," said he, "that I am an *arathmatician*, and I can work it out by the rule of *substraction*, which is a great deal better. But you must all agree to bide by the figures." All having pledged themselves to do so, Pat proceeded. " Well, then—take Paddy from Paddy you can't; but take Dennis from Murphy, and Teague remains. By my soul, Teague, my jewel, and it's you that can't go."

Arithmetic triumphed, and they lost their learned friend Teague. We got the right address for them at last, though it was written in strange characters, and might have been done with the blunt handle of the spade the writer better knew the use of than a pen. Poor fellows, good luck to you! but you'll soon find out that New York streets are not paved with five shilling pieces; nor do the pigs go about ready roasted with a knife and fork stuck in them, crying, " come eat me." Talking of that, we are going to cross here—take care of the pigs; two large sows are trotting up behind this carriage, and a select party of gentlemanly hogs have just turned round the corner.

Here is a melancholy looking swine, lounging homeward by himself; he has only one ear ; he does not go so for fashion's sake you may believe, having parted with the other, very much against his inclination, to some vagrant dogs in the course of his city rambles; but he gets on very well without it, and leads a roving, gentlemanly vagabond kind of life, answering very much to that of " a man about town" in London. Like him he leaves his lodging every morning at a certain hour, throws himself upon the town, gets through his day in some manner quite satisfactory to himself, and regularly appears at the door of his own house at night, and has no need of a latch key to let himself in. He is a free and easy, careless, indifferent kind of pig, having a very large acquaintance amongst other pigs of the same character, whom he rather knows by sight than conversation, as he never troubles himself to stop and exchange civilities, but goes jauntily down the kennels, turning up the news and small talk of the city, in the shape of cabbage stalks and offal, and bearing no *tail* but his own, which is rather short, as the dogs have had sundry nibbles at it, and *cur-tailed* it of its " fair proportions."

What, in heaven's name, are all these people pushing about so hastily—something the matter? We have stopped to speak to six persons, and they have all, after exchanging a few hasty words, bolted off as if shot from a cannon; they are men of business, they have no time for ordinary conversation; every thing here gives way to business.

From the earliest hour in the morning till late at night the streets, offices, and warehouses of the large cities are thronged by men of all trades and professions, each following his vocation like a *perpetuum mobile*, as if he never dreamt of cessation from labour, or the possibility of becoming fatigued. If a lounger should happen to be parading the street, he would be sure to be jostled off the side walk, or be pushed in every direction until he keep time with the rest. Should he meet with a friend he will only talk to him on *business*—on Change they will only hear him on *business*—and if he retire to some house of entertainment he will again be entertained with *business*. Wherever he goes the hum and bustle of *business* will follow him; and when he finally sits down to his dinner, hoping there, at least, to find an hour of rest, he will discover, to his sorrow, that the Americans treat that as a *business*, too, and despatch it in lsss time than he is able to stretch his limbs under the mahogany. In a very few minutes the clang of steel and silver will cease, and he will again be left to his solitary reflections, while the rest are about their *business*. In the evenings, if he have no friends or acquaintance, none will intrude upon his retirement; for the people are either at home with their families, or preparing for the *business* of the next day. Whoever goes to the United States for the purpose of settling there must resolve in his mind to find pleasure in business, and business in pleasure, or he will be disappointed, and wish himself back to the sociable idleness of Europe. Nor can any one travel in the United States without making business of it. In vain would he hope to proceed at his ease; he must prepare to go at the rate of fifteen or twenty miles an hour, or conclude to stay quietly at home. He must not expect to stop, except at the places fixed upon by the proprietors of the road or the steamboat, and if he happens to take a friend by the hand an instant after the sign of departure be given, he is either left behind, or carried on against his intention, and has to inquire after his luggage in another State or territory. The habit of posting being unknown, he is obliged to travel in company with the large caravans which are daily starting from and arriving at all the large cities, under convoy of a thousand puffing and clanking engines, where all thoughts of pleasure are speedily converted into sober reflections on the safety of property and persons. He must resign the gratification of his own individual tastes to the wishes of the majority who are travelling on business, and with whom speed is infinitely more important than all that contributes to pleasure: he must drink, sleep, and wake when they do, and has no other remedy for the catalogue of his distresses but the hope of their speedy termination. Arrived at the period of his sufferings, he must be cautious how he gives vent to his joy, for he must *stop quickly*, if his *busy* conductor shall not hurl him on again on a new journey. Neither is this hurry of business confined to the large cities, or the method of travelling; it communicates itself to every village and hamlet, and extends to, and penetrates the western forests. Town and country rival each other in the eagerness of industrious pursuits. Machines are invented, new lines of communication established, and the depths of the sea explored to afford scope for the spirit of enterprise; and it is as if all America were but one gigantic workshop, over the entrance of which there is the blazing inscription, " *No admission here except on business !*"

But here we are in the New York Alsatia. This is the place—these narrow ways diverging to the right and left, and reeking everywhere with dirt and filth. The lives that are led here bear the same fruits as elsewhere; the coarse and blanched faces at the door have counterparts at home, and, all the wide world over, debauchery has made the very houses prematurely old. Look at the rotten beams, how they are tumbling down, and how the patched and broken windows seem to scowl dimly, like eyes that have received some knocks in a drunken broil. Most of the pigs reside here. Do they ever wonder why their proprietors walk on two legs instead of four, and talk instead of grunt? Nearly every house is a tavern, and in the bar-room are villanous coloured prints of Washington, Queen Victoria, and the American Eagle. Speaking of the Eagle reminds me of a remark made by an English sailor on board the Great Western as we came out to New York; he was arguing with an American tar upon the various merits of England in comparison with those of the United States :—

" But look at our Eagle," said the transatlantic citizen, for even sailors are citizens in America; " there's a bird for you—look at his claws."

" And look at the British Lion," replied the English tar, who was a little mystified by argument and grog; " there's a bird for you; and, talking of claws, I think they've ruffled your bird's feathers before now."

" I guess our Eagle will fly right away with the British Lion, tail and all, next war," answered the American. " I don't wonder you call your place Old England—it is getting cruel crazy."

The Yankees seldom give a chance away in the shape of brag. I heard a capital exemplification of it to-day at the bar of a tavern we entered for some necessary refreshment, for the day was sultry in the extreme. An Englishman was reading a London paper.

" P'r'aps you'll give us a bit of that ?" said a sturdy down-easter, who was seated with his face to the back of the chair, at which he was whittling away with all his might.

The Englishman read a long account of the celebration of the birth-day of some scion of nobility, in which it was mentioned that a bowl of punch was made of such capacious dimensions that a small boat bearing a boy floated on it, and from which he ladled it out to the guests.

" That's nothing," said the Yankee, nearly cutting through the top-rail of the chair in his vehement action of whittling. " When my eldest brother was twenty-one year old, my father cleared out a twelve-foot pond, and filled it with such punch as I guess you never tasted. It was iron strong, I tell you ; and when one or two of the party said it warn't sweet enough, I and two or three more young-un's dived right slick slap to the bottom, and stirred up the sugar !"

As whittling may not be understood by all my readers, I will just mention this custom, which is so common in the eastern states.

It is a habit arising from the natural restlessness of the American, when he is not employed, of cutting a piece of stick or anything else with his knife. Some are so wedded to it from long custom, that, if they have not a piece of stick to cut, they will whittle the backs of the chairs, or anything within their reach. A Yankee, shown into a room to await the arrival of another, has been known to whittle away nearly the whole of the mantel-piece. Lawyers in court whittle away at the table before them, and judges will cut through their own bench. In some courts they put sticks before noted whittlers to save the furniture. The down-easters, as the Yankees are termed generally, whittle when they are making a bargain, as it fills up the pauses, gives them time for reflection, and, moreover, prevents any examination of the countenance ; for in bargaining, like the game of brag, the countenance is carefully watched, as an index to the wishes.

I was once witness to a bargain made between two respectable Yankees, who wished to agree about a farm, and in which whittling was resorted to. They sat down on a log of wood, about three or four feet apart from each other, with their faces turned opposite ways ; that is, one had his legs on one side of the log, with his face to the east, and the other his legs on the other side, with his face to the west. One had a piece of soft wood, and was sawing it with his penknife ; the other had an unbarked hiccory-stick, which he was peeling for a walking-stick.

" Well, good morning—and about this farm ?"

" I don't know ; what will you take ?"

" What will you give ?"

Silence, and whittle away.

" Well, I should think two thousand dollars a heap of money for this farm."

" I have a notion it will never go for three thousand, any how."

" But where's the sun to ripen the corn ?"

" Sun shines on all alike."

" Not exactly through Vermont Hill, I reckon."

" The driver offer me as much as I say, if I recollect right."

" Money not always to be depended upon. Money not always forthcoming."

" I reckon I shall make an elegant 'backy-stopper of this piece of sycamore."

Silence for a few moments. Knives hard at work.

" I have a notion that this is as pretty a hiccory-stick as ever came out of a wood."

" I shouldn't mind two thousand five hundred dollars, and time given."

" It couldn't be more than six months, then, if it goes at that price."
Pause.

" Well, that might suit me."

" What do you say, then ?"

" I suppose it must be so."

" It's a bargain, then—(rising up).   Come, let's liquor on it."

But, having digressed a few moments, let us onward.   What place is this to which the squalid street conducts us ?   A kind of square of leprous houses, some of which are attainable only by crazy wooden stairs without.   What lies beyond this tottering flight of steps—that creak beneath our tread !   A miserable room, lighted by one dim candle, and destitute of all comfort, save that which may be hidden in a wretched bed.   Beside it sits a man, his elbows on his knees, his forehead hidden in his hands.

" What ails that man ?" is asked.

" Fever," he replied, without looking up.

Conceive the fancies of a fevered brain in such a place as this !

Here, too, are lanes and alleys paved with mud, knee-deep ; underground chambers, where they dance and game ; the walls bedecked with rough designs of ships and forts and flags and American eagles out of number ; ruined houses open to the street, whence, through wide gaps in the walls, other ruins loom upon the eye, as though the world of vice and misery had nothing else to show.   Hideous tenements, which take their name from robbery and murder : all that is loathsome, drooping, and decayed is here.

Our guide has his hand upon the latch of " Almack's," and calls us from the bottom of the steps ; for the assembly of the Five Points fashionables is approached by a descent.   Shall we go in ? 'tis but for a moment.

We are welcomed by the landlady, a buxom, fat Mulatto woman, with sparkling eyes, whose head is ornamented with a handkerchief of many colours.   Nor is the landlord behind her in his finery.   He is dressed in a smart blue jacket, like a ship's steward, with a thick gold ring upon his little finger, and round his neck a gleaming golden watch-guard.   How glad he is to see us !   What will we please to call for ?   A dinner.   It shall be done directly, sirs.   A regular break-down.

The corpulent black fiddler, and his friend who plays the tambourine, stamp upon the board of the small raised orchestra, in which they sit and play a lively measure.   Five or six couple come upon the floor, marshalled by a sprightly young negro, who is the wit of the assembly, and the greatest dancer known.   He never leaves off making queer faces, and is the delight of all the rest, who grin from ear to ear incessantly.

Among the dancers are two young Mulatto girls, with large black drooping eyes, and head-gear after the fashion of the hostess, who are as shy, or feign to be, as though they never danced before, and so look down before their visitors, that their partners can see nothing but the long, fringed lashes.

But the dance commences.   Every gentleman sets as long as he likes to the opposite lady, and the opposite lady to him ; and all are so long about it that the sport begins to languish—when suddenly the lively hero dashes in to the rescue.   Instantly the fiddler grins, and goes at it tooth and nail.   There is new energy in the tambourine, new laughter in the dancers, new smiles in the landlady, new confidence in the land-lord, new brightness in the very candles.   Single shuffle, double shuffle, cut and cross cut, snapping his fingers, rolling his eyes, turning in his knees ; presenting the back of his legs in front, spinning about on his toes and heels, like nothing but the man's fingers on the tambourine ; dancing with two left legs, two right legs, two wooden legs, two wire legs, two spring legs, all sorts of legs, and no legs, and finishes by leaping gloriously on the bar-counter, and calling for something to drink, with the chuckle of a million Jim Crows, in one inimitable bound.

      *   *   *   *   *   *

We dined at the City Hotel, and I had an opportunity of observing how the Americans feed in public.   The bell rang, and the guests, to the number of eighty, rushed in like hungry dogs at the call of the kennel keeper.   There was every thing on the table that could be desired. Venison, neat turtle, joints of all kinds, and poultry of all sorts, from the tame fowl to the wild turkey, and rare and delicious canvass backed duck, baked pastry, creams and jellies—all put on the table together.   Every-body helped themselves, and nobody helped any body else, excepting by chance some uninitiated one, who suffered his politeness to spoil his dinner.   All ate as if life and death depended on the meal being finished.   On one gentleman's plate I observed fish, fowl, pickles, and apple tart—a pretty mixture, truly !   But then there's no accounting for taste.   Opposite to me was seated a person whom I thought was mad ; but it turned out at last that he was only *liquored—videlicet, drunk.*

He sat down opposite to me, at the same table.   It appeared as if his *vision was inverted* by the quantity of liquor which he had taken.   Every thing close to him on the table he considered to be out of his reach, whilst everything at a distance he attempted to lay hold of.   He sat up as erect as he could, balancing himself, so as not to appear *corned*, and, fixing his eye upon me, said—

" Sir, I'll trouble you for some fried ham."

Now, the ham was in the dish next to him, and altogether out of my reach.   I told him so.

" Sir," said he again, " as a gentleman, I ask you to give me some of that fried ham."

Amused with the curious demand, I rose from my chair, went round to him, and helped him.

" Shall I give you a potato," said I, the potatoes being at my end of the table, and I not wishing to rise again.

" No, sir," replied he, " I can help myself to them."

He made a dash at them, but did not reach them; then made another and another, till he lost his balance, and lay down upon his plate; this time he gained the potatoes, helped himself, and commenced eating. After a few minutes he again fixed his eyes upon me.

" Sir, I'll trouble you—for the pickles."

They were actually under his nose, and I pointed them out to him.

" I believe, sir, I asked you for the pickles," repeated he, after a time.

" Well, there they are," replied I, wishing to see what he would do.

" Sir, are you a gentleman? As a gentleman—I ask you as a gentleman—for them 'ere pickles."

It was impossible to resist his appeal, so I rose and helped him. I was now convinced that his vision was somehow or another inverted; and to prove it, when he asked me for the salt, which was within his reach, I removed it further off.

" Thank ye, sir," said he, sprawling over the table after it.

I timed the whole party, and in seven minutes, out of the eighty that had sat down to dinner, but eleven remained; the rest had departed. Were they particularly engaged, had they business of importance—no, business is now over, but they have to fulfil another important ceremony, viz., to go outside and sit upon the step, if the weather is fine, and spit upon everybody that comes in and out, or wander backwards and forwards from the bar, take a drink with one, and drink with the other, then another cigar, and then, spit—spit—spit!

" Don't move, General," says one, as his friend bobbed his head a little aside on hearing the preparatory noise of determined expectoration " don't move, General—there, I knew *I could clear you!*"

There's no exaggeration in their spitting propensities, as a proof o which I give an extract from one of their own papers on the interesting subject :—

" English travellers, who have visited this country, all seem to have particularly noticed the propensity which the people of the United States seem to cherish for spitting, and appear to have given much offence by their remarks in relation to this subject. We are inclined, however, to think that they are not exaggerated. The proprietors of the great Exchange Hotel in New Orleans lately sent to Philadelphia for various articles of furniture, and including in the order *three hundred spittoons*—also *twelve extra large spittoons*, thirty-six inches in diameter! It is doubtless the intention of the proprietor of this hotel, that the rooms should be guarded at all points against the ptyalism of the guests. The 'extra large spittoons,' are undoubtedly intended for the accommodation of those who are in the habit of spitting by platoons."—*Boston Gazette.*

This filthy habit is carried to such an excess in every part of the United States, that I am informed that many a determined chewer will not sleep at an inn unless he can have the wall—that is, have his bed so placed that he can, without incommoding himself by rising, spit upon the wall; and it is no uncommon thing to see that portion of the room in such a state as to turn the stomach of any one not accustomed to such sights. An English officer, Colonel A———, was travelling in a stage to New York, and was extremely annoyed by a free and enlightened citizen's perpetually spitting, across him, out of the widow. He bore it patiently for some time, till at last he ventured to remonstrate, when the other said—

" Why, Colonel, I estimate you're poking fun at me—that I do. Now, I'm not agoing to chaw my own bilge-water, not for no man. Besides, you need not look so thundering ugly. Why, I've *practised* all my life, and could squirt through the eye of a needle without touching the steel—let alone such a great saliva box as that there window." Colonel A——— remained tranquil for some time; at last his anger got up, and he spat bang in his companion's face, exclaiming, " I beg you a thousand pardons, squire, but I've not practised as much as you have. No doubt by the time we reach New York I shall be as great a dabster as you are." The other rubbed his eye, and remained with his mouth close shut during the remainder of the journey. The Americans are, in fact, anything but a cleanly people; witness the bed-rooms at most of the small inns, in which you will rarely find the materials for ablution. 'Tis true that in most of the taverns there is in the passage, as near as possible to the eating-room, a jack-towel, a basin, jug with water, and, tied up by a long string, a brush and comb, which all use indiscriminately.

A few minutes previous to the bell ringing for dinner, there is an immense crowding and a splashing noise heard, by parties engaged in what they elegantly term " fixing themselves for dinner," which consists in washing their hands, dry-rubbing their faces, and combing out their hair. I laughed heartily at an account given me to-day of an Englishman who had arrived just in time for dinner, and who gained the washing party previous to entering the room. After washing his hands and face he took a comb and tooth-brush from his pocket, the latter of which he laid down while using the former; turning his head round, attracted by a gurgling noise, he perceived a Yankee in the act of cleansing his teeth with his tooth-brush.

" I beg your pardon, sir," said he, " but that is my brush."

" Don't mention it," answered the Yankee, " hav'n't hurt it," giving it a rinse through the water, " thought it belonged to the house !"

On leaving the hotel, I witnessed a singular effect produced by the most simple means, which may possibly be a secret worth knowing, and important to horsemen. Just as we left the door, the Yankee who had been my companion on ship-board, came up and accosted me—

" Glad to see you," said he; " got all right I guess. How do you like our country, eh? Hav'n't got a street like this in London I calculate ?—awful lengthy, ain't it, eh ?"

As we happened to be passing in the front of the United States Hotel, we observed a large crowd attracted by an omnibus laden with passengers, which the horses refused to draw. The driver had tried every expedient to urge on the animals—such as the ordinary modes of whipping, coaxing, &c., but all in vain, when the Yankee suggested the plan of tying a string tightly round the horses' ears close to the head. The driver apprehending that he was disposed to quiz him, refused to make the trial, but upon the Yankee tying the twine round the horses' ears—having requested the driver to resume his seat and to give the horses a loose rein, without applying the whip—it operated like a charm, and the animals started off without further difficulty, to the infinite amusement and gratification of the bystanders; he then stated to the crowd, that he had tried the experiment more than a hundred times, and had never known it to fail but once, and then, said he, it was a cursed cross-grained mare, and she wouldn't be fixed no how, and he commenced explaining to the crowd how and where he obtained his knowledge, apparently excessively proud of his feat.

If I was asked to describe the American as far only as I saw him at New York, I should say he was a spitting and oyster-eating animal. Oysters—stewed, fried, and roasted—are to be met with in every street; and "Take an oyster?" is a question as common as take a drink or take a cigar. In fact, there is something humanising in the proffer. In no other place in the world is such a question asked. In Holland they ask you to drink schnapps—in England, to take a dram; but no one asks you to beef with him. In America, although there is no lack of proffers of the liquid refreshment, they have the decency to consider that it may be taken on empty intestines, and the proffered oyster, as a plaster to the wounded stomach, shows some kindly consideration. That the Americans are a generous and hospitable people there is not the remotest doubt. There is, to use one of their own phrases, " Nothing mean about me;" and their great horror of being considered sponging, or importunate on any occasion, is strongly manifested.

Their expression of disgust at a person who is considered selfish is very powerful and characteristic.—" Well, he is the meanest white man I ever saw!" or, " Such a one is meaner than the little end of nothing whittled down!" In fact, with all their faults and eccentricities, they are a bold and generous people. Let them talk to you, question and cross-question you, and you win their hearts; and they are no niggards of information as regards themselves, for you need not be in the society of an American an hour before you may learn where he was *raised—fotched-up*—and educated!

Glad to escape from this scene I now took a quiet stroll on the Battery; 'tis a splendid sight; the distant shores of Jersey, the mouth of the glorious Hudson, the distant view of Staten Island, the bright waters dotted with the white sails, all looks fresh, new, and exciting. We leave the Battery. What church is this?—'tis St. Paul's; here is the tomb of the celebrated George Frederick Cooke, and here two lowly graves which contain the mouldering remains of two humble individuals whose story is worth hearing. Let us return to our inn— now light the candles, and now let us fancy some of our English comforts, and now your story.

CHAPTER IV.

" In May's sweet month, or June's more balmy hour,
I puff my meerschaum still in shady bower,
Or stroll with it where scented hawthorns breathe,
Or by some green tree watch its vapours wreathe,
More calm the pleasure, then, its influence lends,
When with sweet summer's flowers its fragance blends.
                                                    ANON.

THE LAST PIPE.

IN a bye street leading from the Broadway still exists a small tavern, yclept the Toby Philpot. I am about to speak of it as it stood ten years since, as my story has reference to that date.   The landlord was then a jolly Englishman, who in person bore a striking resemblance to the portrait displayed at his door of that celebrated bon-vivant, previous to his transmutation into a brown jug, so beautifully described in the ballad with which all are familiar.

He was a native of Hampshire, on the coast of which he had long maintained a profitable trade, until a slight difference of opinion with those obnoxious persons on whom devolved the duty of collecting his Majesty's excise induced him to cross the Atlantic, and try his calling in a land unencumbered with those pests of innkeepers—coast-guards, revenue-officers, and prying guagers !

He had been many years proprietor of the house in question, a domicile of ancient standing ; testifying, by the yellow bricks, low porch, and gable ends, its Dutch extraction.   The parlour, a large room occupying nearly the whole ground-floor, had assumed, under his arrangement (in contradistinction to all other American taverns), the snug and comfortable appearance found only in an English public-house. The large bay-windows, one of which looked into a quiet street, and the other over a well trimmed garden, rendered it a cool and agreeable retreat in summer ; and on a winter's evening, when the red damask curtains were closed, and a fire blazed in the capacious grate (for stoves, and the use of wood, were eschewed by the hearth of the Toby Philpot) was anything but an unpleasant location for those of a country proverbial for their love of ease, and a sea-coal fire.

There was an exclusiveness in the society frequenting this apartment, all the appointments of which were decidedly anti-American; on the walls hung no representation of the immortal Washington, in the usual tea-pot attitude in which it has pleased the artist invariably to place him. No gilt frame enclosed that celebrated declaration, dictated by those immaculate worthies who forgot their black brethren in the announcement of freedom and equality to all! but, in their place, in full Windsor uniform, his most Gracious Majesty George the Fourth, blandly smiled upon the hero of the Nile, issuing, from the opposite side of the room, his memorable mandate which secured for ever the ocean-supremacy of England! A few portraits of winning horses, and Hogarth's "Rake's Progress" completed the pictorial department. The great attraction of the house was the excellent ale brewed by the proprietor, an article no where else attainable; and which, served in bright pewter measures, with the huge tobacco-box and long pipes, at every other establishment either exploded or unknown, blended with the composed and social air of its frequenters, so admirably contrasted with the hurried, restless, and uncompanionable drinking of the Americans, threw around it that truly English appearance which the afflicted by the "maladie du-pays," (to which the natives of London are especially liable,) might, by a slight effort of imagination, fancy themselves transported to some favourite haunt, or suburban retreat, in the "giant city" of their affection.

Here the temporary sojourner might indulge in those criticisms on trans-atlantic character and manners, not generally politic in mixed American society; but woe to the stray native who, incautiously penetrating its arcanum, ventured any of those witty allusions to the naval and military superiority of his country, with which they are too often wont to indulge their visitors; here he very soon found himself in a fearful minority; for whatever little personal quarrel they might have had with the laws of their native land, and although no reciprocity might exist between them, the pure flame of loyalty, and ardent love of country, was nowhere, on all occasions, more loudly demonstrated, than by mine host himself, and the truly English frequenters of the Toby Philpot!

Many a missing man, mourned, but not forgotten, by creditors and friends in England, it has been my lot to meet under that hospitable roof; although, for some important reasons, still maintaining an imperfect incognito: here might be occasionally encountered one of those incautious speculators well known at Lloyd's, whose name was at one time a sufficient guarantee for thousands upon the Stock Exchange, driven by the base ingratitude of friends, or the villanous conspiracy of his compatriots, to sip his humble ale with mine host of the Toby, under the assumed denomination of Brown, Jones, or Robinson; wishing, with a kind feeling worthy of better fortunes, his presence his attractive domicile! The sound lawyer, disgusted with the trickery and procrastination of the English courts, previously erasing his name from the iniquitous "roll" of British practitioners, found in the simpler jurisprudence of the land he had adopted, more congenial employment, and in the society of the Toby Philpot a correspondent relief from its cares! The medical adviser, who, taking a liberal view of his divine might excite neither awe nor restraint in the humbler frequenters of art, had scorned the beaten track of his contemporaries, gifted with the knowledge of a panacea of universal efficacy, derided by the mis-named faculty of England, had the satisfaction, in its general accepta-tion by a more enlightened community, of finding his benevolent efforts appreciated; and amidst kindred souls, in this convivial circle of his countrymen abroad, condolence for the unjust aspersions cast upon his fame by the envious and malignant at home!

Such were the more aristocratic visitors that occasionally graced the domicile of mine host; but my story has reference to two individuals of a humbler class, who, every evening, occupied two particular chairs, from habit long considered exclusively their own, at one extremity of the large oval table in the parlour of the Toby Philpot. For upwards of seven years they had invariably met at nine o'clock, and as regularly departed at the sober hour of eleven; they generally entered the house at the same moment, although coming immediately from their respective employments at distant and opposite quarters of the city, and constantly left it together; not, however, from any idea of companion-ship, for they instantly parted at the door with a familiar nod, which, with them, answered, apparently, all purpose of conversation and adieus: so extraordinary was the taciturnity of both, "to be as dumb as Ben Brooks," or "as silent as Jem Walters," was proverbial amongst the frequenters of the room; the politics of the mother-country, discussed with all the vehement interest of the absentee, had for them, appa-rently, no charm; and if accidentally appealed to for an opinion, it was, on all occasions, given after the guarded fashion of Lord Burleigh, as described in the admirable farce of the *Critic*. Inveterate smokers of the olden school, they steadily adhered to the long clay pipe, and lamented, in dumb show, the falling off of the members of the Saturday-night club; every individual of which, themselves excepted, had gradually adopted the more modern and convenient *cigar*. That a strong and mutual friendship existed between them was demonstrated in the placid enjoyment each seemed to derive from the immediate proximity of the other, and in the little familiar colloquy which con-stantly prefaced its indulgence; although, when the interrogation of "is your pipe alight, Jem?" had been made, and the ambiguous and guarded reply of "all right, Ben," responded, (the whole extent of conversation, nightly unvaried in its repetition, they were ever known publicly to indulge in,) an indifferent observer might have imagined them perfect strangers.

There was a respectability about the quiet inseparables, which had won them the consideration and esteem of all; their silent habits rendered them anything but disagreeable companions; and as talkers are always most numerous in mixed society, the loquaciously inclined could always calculate upon, at least, two excellent listeners; their laugh was always ready, let the jest be ever so stale; and on the conclusion of a jovial song, or a call for its repetition, no individuals of the society thumped the substantial table with heartier good will, than Ben and his companion. The latter indeed, on all occasions, seemed to take the cue from his friend; on the clock proclaiming the hour of eleven, it was Ben who gave the quiet signal of departure, without which, it had been proved, the other would have continued enveloped in his smoky panoply until the morning; as, on one occasion, when sleep had overpowered his monitor, he was observed to take no note of time, until the waiter awoke the slumberer, for the purpose of informing him that the establishment was about closing.

From mine host I learned some particulars of their history; they had commenced life together as friendless boys, were apprenticed from a London parochial establishment to the same country town, Ben to a farmer, and his companion to a blacksmith. They each served their time, and continued some years with their respective masters, when a judicious marriage with a worthy helpmate, placed a small sum of money at the disposal of Ben, in addition to the savings of a few years of labour. Allured by a flattering description of the Western El Dorado, he resolved to embark his fortunes, in conjunction with others equally experienced in such matters as himself, in one of those visionary speculations set forth by a party of unprincipled and rapacious adventurers. Little solicitation induced his early friend to join him, whose habits of frugality enabled him to do so without becoming a burthen to his companion; and with the wife of his bosom on the one side, and the friend of his heart on the other, he prepared, without those regrets which accompany the man of happier fortune, to leave the land of his nativity, to which neither had been bound, from their earliest years, by any ties of consanguinity.

Continued delays of the voyage, and other unforeseen circumstances had, on their arrival at their destination, considerably diminished their little store; and a few months' residence in an unhealthy climate, proved the fallacy on which they had founded their expectations of fortune. The death of Ben's wife in child-birth, and a severe illness which deprived him (who was alone acquainted with agricultural matters) of all exertion, put the finishing stroke to their misfortunes; and at the end of a year from their arrival in the Illinois territory, they found themselves reduced to comparative indigence.

With many a bitter tear shed on the lonely forest grave of his wife and infant, poor Ben and his companion prepared to leave the scene of their misfortunes; and after enduring every misery and privation, made their way from the Western wilderness to New York, in the hope of obtaining employment, or the means of returning to England.

Their first and, indeed, only friend was mine host of the Toby, through whose influence Jem, who was an excellent workman, found the means of supporting for some months both himself and companion.   Ben was soon afterwards engaged by an horticulturist at a short distance from the city, to whose business, after a lapse of time, he succeeded; and for many years prosperity had followed their mutual exertions.

Whether their taciturnity had been contracted amongst the Indians with whom, during their wandering, they had made a temporary sojourn, or was constitutional, I am not aware; but mine host, with whom they were on terms of intimacy, seldom elicited more than monosyllables; and in no one instance had they been known publicly to depart from those silent habits which rendered them so peculiar.

On Sunday, the only day they could enjoy together, they might be seen occupying, both at morning and evening service, an humble seat in the aisle of St. Paul's church, or walking on the Battery, gazing complacently on the wide waters which separated them from the home of their childhood, endeared by no sweet remembrance of parental affection or bonds of kindred.   Apparently content with their present lot, each had sought no other tie; and, ludicrous as their habits, in the only society they ever mixed in, might appear to the indifferent observer, I felt with others, who knew their story, a respect for the deep and holy friendship which evidently existed between the quiet and lonely inseparables, who still continued to take their accustomed seats at the large oval table, when the usual interrogation and reply closed the conversational part of the evening.

The winter of 1829 set in with unusual severity, about the middle of which Ben and his companion were missed for some weeks in the parlour of the Toby Philpot!   Various conjectures and surmises were afloat amongst its visitors, when, on a Saturday evening, as the members of the smoking club had just commenced their fumitory operations, precisely on the stroke of nine, Ben glided quietly into the room; he was alone, and his sombre garb testified at once he was companionless.   Taking his accustomed seat, he put his lips mechanically to the ale placed before him, lit his pipe, now the only "light of other days," and commenced his usual interrogation.   Glancing wildly on the vacant chair, from which no wonted reply was returned, he was recalled at once to his lonely situation; a tear stole down his cheek, as the remembrance of all their mutual suffering passed in review before him, when, hiding his emotion in quick and hasty puffs, he received, but without reply, the condolence of the room on his bereavement.   At the accustomed hour he arose to depart, but seemed involuntarily to linger, as if for his companion.

Day after day it was distressing to witness the efforts of this lonely man to suppress the habits of years; whilst his pale cheek and wasting frame gave sure presage of approaching dissolution.   Weeks passed away, and a spell seemed cast over the hilarity of the parlour of the Toby Philpot by the spectral appearance of Ben and his long pipe; a sad and silent man, he continued to glide into his usual seat at the accustomed time, and vanish gloomily at the eleventh hour!

Business at this time took me from the city, and on my return after a short absence, I hastened to the accustomed haunt. It was ten o'clock when I entered the room. A change had taken place; the huge tobacco-box, and tray containing the obsolete instruments of smoking, no longer graced the oblong table. Mine host, seated in the accustomed place of the melancholy Ben, was relating his fate; I caught but the

conclusion of his narrative. "Yes," said he, with a sigh, gulping down the remains of a glass of brandy and water, "poor Ben's gone; never got over Jem's death; his light's out—good creature—never used *no bad language.*" It was too true; the inseparables were reunited in death! The grim king of terrors had extinguished the last pipe of the Toby Philpot!

CHAPTER V.

" I'll tell thee what, thou thin man in a censer, we'll have you as soundly swinged
for this, you blue-bottle rogue, you filthy, famished correctioner ; if you be not hanged
I'll forswear half kirkles."

SHAKSPERE.

" As to starved wretch, without a penny piece,
  Is the broad point, all shining and all grease,
Of place 'yclept cook-shop !"

ANON.

THIS morning I devoted to a view of the New York courts of justice.
The absence of the ceremonials in England certainly detracts much
from the effect of the thing after all.   There is " Wisdom in the wig,"
and the gown of the counsellor gives a something of importance which
is but befitting the occasion.   Let us listen to this case.   The prisoner
is arraigned for stealing six quarts of cyder.   The thing is proved
against him clear as day ; but his counsellor, of course, has a right to be
heard.   Now hear a specimen of Yankee eloquence.   He rises slowly, first
removing a plug of tobacco from his mouth, and then delivers himself
of the following—

" GENTLEMEN OF THE JURY—It is with feelings of no ordinary
commotion that I rise to defend the character of my injured client from
the attacks which have been made upon his heretofore unapproachable
character.   I feel, gentlemen, that, though a good deal smarter than
any of you are, or even the Judge here, yet that I am totally incom-
petent to present this ere case in that magnanimous and heart-rendering
light which its importance demands.   And I trust, gentlemen, that
whatever I may lack in presenting the subject, will be immediately
made up by your own good sense and discernment, if you have any.

" The counsel for the prosecution, gentlemen, will undoubtedly en-
deavour to heave dust in your eyes : he will tell you that his client is a
man of function—that he is a man of unimpeachable voracity—that he
is a man who would scorn to fotch an action against another merely to

gratify his personal corporosity; but let me retreat you, gentlemen, to beware how you rely upon any spacious reasoning like this, I myself apprehended that this ere suit has been wilfully and maliciously fotcht— fotcht, gentlemen, for the sole and only purpose of browbeating my unhappy client here, and in an eminent manner grinding the face of the poor; and, gentlemen, I apprehend that, if you could look into that man's heart, and read the motives that propelled him to fotch this suit, such a pictur of moral turpentine and heartfelt ingratitude would be brought to light as has never before been experienced since the Fall of Niagara.

"Now, gentlemen, I want to make a brilliant appeal to the kind sympathies of your nater, and see if I can't warp your judgment a little in favour of my unfortunate client, and then I shall fotch my arrangements to a close. Here is a poor man, who has a numerous wife and children dependent on him for their daily bread and butter, wantonly fotcht up here, and arranged before an intellectual jury, on the charge of eggnomiously hooking—yes, gentlemen, mark the idea—hooking six quarts of cider. You, gentlemen, have all been placed in the same situation, and you know how to feel for the misfortunes of my heartbroken client; and I hope you will not permit the natural gushings of your sympathising heart to be overcome by the superstitious arguments of my ignorant opponent on the other side. The law expressly declares, gentlemen, in the language of Shakspere, that wher no doubt exists of the guilt of a prisoner, it is your duty to lean upon the side of justice, and fotch him in innocent, If you keep this fact in view, you will have the honour, gentlemen, of making a friend of him and all his relations; and you can allers look back upon this, kase that you did as you have been done by. But if you disregard this point of law, set at naught my eloquent remarks, and fotch him in guilty, the silent twitches of conscience will foller you over every fair cornfield, and my injured client, gentlemen, will be pretty apt to light on you some of these dark nights, as my cat lights on a saucer full of new milk."

Loud bursts of approbation followed this speech; and the prisoner was honourably acquitted!

The next case is a nigger—or rather, as they love to be termed, a coloured person. He is charged with a serious assault, for which he has already been imprisoned two months, previous to his trial. It appears that, in passing up Broadway, he ran against the umbrella of a free and enlightened citizen, the point of which entered his eye, and the violence of the shock destroyed the perpendicular of the white man.

The counsel of the plaintiff descanted, in a most incontrovertible style, upon the evils of the abolition of slavery, and proved clearly to the Judge, that if Joe Shink, the free and independent nigger, had been working in a rice-field in North Carolina, he couldn't have assaulted an independent citizen in New York.

Sentence, Six months to the prison at Sing-Sing, where, with his woolly head half-shaved, Joe Shink was soon employed in sawing stone —a very pretty employment in summer: so much for justice. But here we are, at the New York Court for the recovery of small debts; precisely the same as our Court of Requests. What case is this just called? Oh, a cookshop-keeper *versus* a Yankee seaman. The defendant in this case, one Saul Tunks, a tall gander-shanked Yankee seaman, belonging to one of the American line of packet ships, lying in the east slip. The plaintiff is a soup and eating-house keeper, residing in Wall-street. The sum sought to be recovered being 2s. 4d. The plaintiff was a punchy little man, some four feet six in his high-lows, with a pair of cheeks that seemed to be distended by means of a couple of apple dumplings. Saul Tunks, on the other hand, was a regular Long Tom Coffin, six feet high at least, with a mouth extending nearly from ear to ear, and as much flesh on his bones as might be found on the mainmast of his ship. The Yankees are all lean, herring-gutted chaps. Though immense feeders, they do not improve upon it, They may " laugh" as much as they like, but " growing fat" is out of the question. A twenty-stone Yankee would be a sight for gods and men— a *rara avis in terris*, and no mistake.

Commissioner (addressing the defendant) : Pray, what are you?

Defendant : Why, I guess, I'm a free and independent citizen of the state of Alabama.

Commissioner : You are an American sailor, I apprehend.

Defendent (giving an impudent leer at the commissioner) : You're a cute chap, old Four-eyes, may I be *lynched* with hot brimstone and porkepine's quills if you arn't. I guess I *am* a sailor, and a ginooine " yellow flower of the forest." (Laughter.)

The behaviour of the defendant in the court was not marked with that decorum which characterises an Englishman in a court of justice. He kept whistling and humming tunes all the time, and addressed the bench with the same familiarity as he would speak to his shipmates. One of the commissioners, who wore spectacles, he dubbed " Old Four-eyes," and another, whose nose resembled in colour the rose more than the lily, he addressed as " Old Copper Conk." Probably this was owing to the notions of *liberty* and *equality* engendered by a republican form of government.

" Three fours of biled beef, three breads, and three plates of taters, is eighteenpence," said the little fat man, calculating ; " and three basins of hox-tail and one bread is tenpence more, which makes altogether 2s. 4d., your honour."

Commissioner : Do you mean to say that he devoured this all at one time?

Defendant : Nowt (nothing) very strange in that, I guess. You never seed my brother Aaron eat, I calculate ; he does the thing " slick," I'm thinking. Aaron, when he arn't been out in the woods, to whet his appetite, puts away four dozen duck eggs for breakfast, a cold goose for lunch, a leg of mutton for dinner, and a gallon of bean soup for supper. But, when Aaron is very hungry, and begins to eat, he can't leave off, no how, 'cause, d'ye see, it arn't in the natur of the hanimal, and his wife has to tie his hands behind him. (Laughter.)

Commissioner : I have heard of many people who, when they begin *talking*, are not able to leave off, but I never heard of any one, except your brother Aaron, who, when he began to *eat*, could not leave off. I suppose he is a sort of human porpoise ?

Defendant : Just the other way, I guess. Aaron's so tarnation thin that a chap with good eyes may see to read the newspaper through him, It arn't the pigs that swallows the most wash gits the fattest.

The plaintiff, in continuation, stated that Saul Tunks stalked into his " slap-bang" establishment, looking as hungry as a pauper, and asked what he could have to eat. Upon receiving a verbal detail of the bill of fare, he chose a basin of oxtail and a " bread;" two basins more finished his first course, and he then put away three plates of " biled beef," as the purveyors of this substantial condiment invariably term it, with the usual complement of " breads" and " taters." After disposing of these, the little fat man thought it was high time to look after the money ; he therefore politely called the attention of Mr. Saul Tunks to an inscription on a small board over the mantel-piece, which set forth, that, in order to " prevent mistakes," gentlemen had better " pay on delivery." Saul heeded not this *gentle* hint, but stretching out his long legs with an air of republican *nonchalance*, he informed the punchy dispenser of " ox-tail" that he would see him d—d before he would pay him a single cent, as the soup was bad, and had disordered his stomach. At length, having discovered what ship he belonged to, the plaintiff allowed him to depart, and summoned him for the money.

Saul, in defence, said that he was taking a stroll, when he suddenly felt " tarnation wolfish," and seeing a vast deal of smoke and steam issuing from the plaintiff's premises, he concluded that he should be able to satisfy his appetite there, and accordingly walked in ; " but the grub," the defendant added, " was tarnation queer ; so, I guess, I don't pay a solitary cent," said Saul.

Commissioner : Pray, what was the matter with the victuals, for you seem to have devoured a tolerable quantity of it ?"

Defendant : Why, I found some sage and ingun in the ox-tail soup, an' I guess that's quite enough to turn the stomach of an alligator. I calculate if he'd been a settler in the free and independent state of Alabama he'd have got " *lynched*" elegant.

The plaintiff assured the Court that if any portion of the defendant's " ox-tail" was flavoured with sage and onion, it must have been caused by the ladle from the roast pork dish being used by mistake.

Defendant : I say, old Roly-poly, can you make a saw-dust pudding ?

Plaintiff : Never heerd of such a thing.

Defendant : Well, I calculate you New York chaps *are* ignoramuses. I guess I'm Saul Tunks, the ginooine " yellow flower of the forest," an' I guess I fed on saw-dust puddings more than a month.

This assertion was looked upon as an out-and-out Jonathan, but Saul assured the Commissioners that it was true. He stated that he once kept a store in the Canadas, where it is customary, previous to the frost setting in, to kill a sufficiency of meat, poultry, &c., to last the winter season. This is stowed away in a cellar, and in a short time becomes so hard from the effect of the intense frost, that it is necessary to use a saw to dissever the joints of meat, and the saw-dust made on these occasions makes an excellent pudding. The above receipt for a saw-dust pudding is a novelty in its way.

Commissioner : Well, after duly considering this matter, we are of opinion that you have no just ground for refusing to pay the money ; we shall, therefore, make an order upon you for the payment of the debt and costs immediately.

Defendant : Well, I guess that's tarnation hard lines. I'll tell you what it is, Master Roly-poly (addressing the plaintiff), if I ever catches you in the free and independent state of Alabama, look out for " Lynch-law."

The " yellow flower of the forest" paid the money and stalked out of Court.

As we came out of Court, my friend was seized upon by a very corpulent gentleman, who expressed great pleasure at seeing him. I was introduced in due form to him : Mr. Barnaby Breakspear, Mr. Stretch, the talented " Buz," and the no less illustrious delineator of the immortal Bard of Avon. We shook hands, bowed, and smiled, like kindred spirits whose hearts were too full for words.

" Haven't a moment to spare," said the New York theatrical manager and dictator, for it was no less a person ; " I dine at three. Bring your friend—too happy—long talk—go to the theatre afterwards ;" and Barnaby Breakspear again shook hands, bowed, smiled, and broke away with the velocity of a fourteen-pounder.

" One of the pleasantest fellows in the world, that," remarked my friend ; " we'll dine with him."

We then walked into Niblo's, and, calling for some port wine sangaree, sat down to rest awhile.

" I'll tell you a story about Barnaby Breakspear," said my friend ; " it will give you an idea of what sort of man he is. He lives like an emperor, and yet he never pays anybody a cent, excepting when, as in the case I am about to relate, he can't help himself. He has been manager of all the theatres in the Union, and this circumstance occurred at Salem, in Massachusetts."

THE RECOVERED TREASURY.

KOTZEBUE, in his admirable drama of the Stranger, makes his heroine exclaim, after expatiating upon the regularity of her weekly employment—" And I often say to myself, is Saturday come again so soon ?" And such was the periodical exclamation of Barnaby Breakspear, manager and proprietor of the pretty theatre at Salem, Massachusetts, excepting that, instead of addressing the wondering ejaculation to his own ponderous person, he invariably applied it to the members of his theatrical company, who regularly claimed on that day the payment of their weekly salaries, more elegantly and properly denominated, " the inefficient reward of merit."

Seated in a small apartment, which served as a dressing-room at night, and appropriated during the day as a room of business, was Barnaby and his treasurer. It was Saturday, and he was engaged in arranging and counting the materiel by which he was enabled to carry on the dramatic war. Theatrical business had lately been but indifferent in the quiet town of Salem. The treasury had become awfully diminished, and each week the sum paid to each talented member was " curtailed of its fair proportions;" and on the important morning our story commences, like the ghost of the poisoned Dane, " *the thing* had not appeared" at all!

Barnaby took his seat as usual, attended by his official. As each actor entered the apartment he reiterated his hackneyed expression of surprise at the sixth day having, by some strange fatality, rushed prematurely forward upon the wings of time. He lamented the hopelessness of his fortunes—the utter prostration of his resources—" told a flattering tale" of hopes in perspective; and, having dismissed each hungry claimant, pocketed the remainder of the week's receipts—too small to divide amongst so many—jumped into his gig, and his celebrated fasttrotting gray horse bore him to Boston time enough to take his seat at a grand turtle dinner at Gallagah's hotel.

A consultation was held on his departure by the dramatis personæ, which, if more noisy than the Indians' councils, had at least two points of great resemblance ; for, if not from the calumet of peace, a prodigious mass of smoke was displayed on the occasion, and no inconsiderable quantity of rum and brandy " drunk upon the *premises.*"

The conduct of Barnaby Breakspear was canvassed with all *that kind feeling and forbearance to the absent which characterises the theatrical profession,* and the meeting adjourned to a neighbouring nine-pin ground. After coming to a fixed and firm determination, that, as they saw no immediate means to extricate themselves from the situation the base conduct of the manager had placed them in, the only way in which they could express the thorough disgust and indignation generally felt, for such conduct was quietly, calmly, and contemptuously to put up with it !

On the following Monday, an engagement for three nights was announced, as having, with considerable expense, and great personal exertion on the part of the manager, concluded with " Signor Chikanis," who was advertised to swallow fire, go into an oven whilst a shoulder of mutton was being baked for his supper ; and to conclude by performing in an entire new piece, in which he would enact, in addition to eight others, the extreme opposite parts of a blue-bottle and an elephant !

All was bustle and excitement in the sober town of Salem, and for three nights the theatre was literally crammed. Barnaby was in high glee, jested, laughed, and chuckled ; and his performers looked forward with longing delight for the approaching Saturday, which, although terminating the season, to them at any rate could not come too soon.

The important morning arrived, and Barnaby was seated at his post. On the table stood the iron box marked "treasury." But the horror of the company can only be imagined when informed that the immense sums taken during the star's engagement would barely supply the means of paying one week's salary, which was given to each claimant. The long arrears were slightly hinted at ; and as the vacation of the company would be but three weeks, promises were liberally made of after remuneration.

On the close of the Salem theatre it was hinted to some of the company that Barnaby Breakspear had declined all further management of that establishment, and those who looked to obtain any remuneration for past services, would most probably have to seek him some thousand miles from that pleasant location, he having entered into a speculation in the far west, whither it was also stated it was his intention immediately to transport himself.

A plan was now arranged by the company, who determined to ascertain whether the defalcation in the payment of their arrears arose from poverty or disinclination. Barnaby was engaged at a dinner on the Saturday, and they were aware it would be late before he started with his treasurer, as was his custom, on his return to Boston.

They met accordingly at a small public house on the high road, about two miles from the town ; each party prepared a disguise, and they resolved to stop the delinquent manager just on the brow of a steep hill, where he must necessarily breath his horse. If he had no money, why it would be but a frolic ; but if the black iron box, marked 'Treasury' was to be found about his person, they determined, then and there, to ascertain its contents. Barnaby, flushed with wine, came rolling along the hard turnpike road, his feet resting in the individual depository, as he walked his fast grey up the hill, and on its summit found himself surrounded by a fierce banditti. One seized his reins, another (the harlequin of the theatre dressed as a brigand) mounted the horse, and presented his carbine full in the face of the astonished director ; another, adorned with a pair of buffalo horns, and dragging a heavy chain, ascended the vehicle and demanded his money.

He offered his purse, for resistance was useless, and Barnaby was not a fighting man.

" What's in this box ?" said a horrid voice, through a ship's trumpet.

" Nothing but papers," replied the agitated treasurer, who was seated beside his employer.

" We must search your papers, then," continued the speaker. " The key—the key."

The key was given, the box opened, and found to be literally full of dollars.

Each robber now removed his mask, and " pay us our arrears," resounded from the united voices of the talented company of the Salem Theatre.

Poor Barnaby had no resource ; it was night, the moon shed her dim light over a strong band of opposers ; and, with trembling hand, he distributed from the iron-bound box the several demands of each performer, who returned to town rejoicing at the success of their scheme, and made a jovial night with the receipts of the

Recovered Treasury !

" Such is the story of the recovered treasury." said my friend, " and Barnaby is sore upon the subject to this day. But come, 'tis on the stroke of three, and we'll be off to dinner."

We found the manager awaiting us. Niblo's establishment for dinners is the most *recherché* place in New York ; and we sat down to a repast that a London alderman might envy. A magnificent dessert followed—pine apples, and all the most delicious preserved fruits were there, and wine which had been three times round the Cape. But all the delicacies were nothing to the racy conversation of Barnaby Breakspear. I have met men of conversational powers of all kinds and grades, but he surpassed them all; no subject was started but he had his *bon mots,* or illustrative anecdotes ready.

" What a splendid pair of black eyes that barmaid has below," said my friend to the manager.

" Talking of eyes," replied he, " I once saw a blind man with three and, stranger still, they were all different colours. I'll tell you how it was :——

" ' I was staying last summer in Kentucky, and I lodged in a farm house, the proprietor of which was as gay and jolly a fellow as ever emptied a whisky jug. Now you must know, in that part of the country they fight rather savagely ; it is the custom there when you have your man down to keep him down, and get his eyes out as soon as you can, which is managed by twisting one finger in the ' gouge lock,' a piece of hair left long on purpose, and insinuating your thumb between the cheek bone and the eye socket. Jabez Proudfoot, my landlord, was esteemed one of the best hands in a regular kick and biting fight in all Kentucky ; he had lost one eye and a small bit of his nose, saving which he was as good-looking a fellow as you'd see in a summer's day. Well, while I was stopping there, a horse fair took place at a village, about four miles from the house ; just as he was mounting his nag to be there early in the morning, I heard the following little colloquy betwixt him and his wife.

" I tell you what it is Jabez, and no mistake," said the wife, " if you go to that ere fair, you're a lost man."

" I guess you're crazy, woman," replied he; " I rather think it wouldn't be easy for me to lose myself between here and Twyfield, any how."

" I don't mean that ; I mean you'll lose your blessed eyesight ; you've only got one eye, remember, and nine babies, and what's to become of me and them if you are in the dark all the rest of your life, I should like to know ?"

" Now look here, gal, I tell ye I won't get into any row, no how ; so don't make yourself ugly about it."

"Well, now don't—but just come slick home, and don't get a *drinking.*"

"Well, well, I won't; there, good bye; and now go-ahead, steamer;' and, so saying, Jabez gave his horse the spur, and dashed off in gallant style for Twyfield fair.

"It was late when he returned, in company with two friends who had undertaken the task of guiding him; for Jabez had, first got *a liquoring,* then *a fighting,* and *a gouging;* and it had ended as his wife had foretold; he had returned home, to use the figurative language of his friends, "without a *drop of eye!*"

"What will become of my precious babes?" cried the wife, wringing her hands, distractedly.

"Never mind, old gal," said Jabez, who was a real pluckt one, "I've got my eye."

"Where?" asked his wife.

"In my waistcoat pocket," said he, proceeding to search for the missing article.

"That's not your eye," said his wife, as he threw one on the table; "nor that either," as another was produced, "nor that," as he fished out a third, "your'n was a blue eye, and these are all black."

"Well, then," exclaimed Jabez, "I hav'n't got it. Give me a drink; I'm darned if I hav'n't picked up the wrong eyes."

Though I could not help laughing at this story, which was well told by Barnaby, who declared it to be a fact, I remarked that the situation of the poor widow should have moved his compassion.

"So it did," said he, "but Jabez Proudfoot moved himself afterwards. Things got rather bad with him; bills became due, and he had no money to meet them with; so, one fine night, he took a moonlight flit down the Mississippi. Perhaps," continued he, " you never heard how they move there?" I expressed my ignorance with due humility.

"Well," resumed Barnaby, "I'll tell you. Jabez had lots of friends, and in eight hours (mind ye, his place was close on the river's bank) they had down houses, stables, barn, and all, made up with the timbers a pretty considerable raft, put themselves and all their timber and live-stock upon it, and before night they were going ahead down the Mississippi above nine knots an hour. Unfortunately, they had not got above twenty miles when they caught a *snag*; but you don't know what a snag is, I suppose?"

Again I confessed that I had left off before I came to that portion of my American education.

"Well, then," continued the narrator, "a snag is a tree which grows in the bed of the river, and as the Mississippi often changes its course, there are plenty of them. Poor Jabez's raft struck slap against one, and in less than no time the raft, the timber, the live-stock, including his wife, were sucked up by the foaming current, and never rose again."

"And what became of Jabez?" inquired I.

"Why, it was never known exactly. He was drowned, no doubt;

but when last seen by a steamer that was passing, he was striking out for dear life, and singing a part of our national anthem, with a slight alteration :—

> " Hail Columbia ! happy land—
> *If I ain't bursted I'll be damn'd!*"

This was the end of poor Jabez Proudfoot, and he informed me that such moves on the Mississippi are by no means uncommon the river; being extremely rapid in its downward course renders it a very expeditious means of conveyance. There is another danger besides the *snag*, termed a *sawyer*, which is also a tree so loosened at its root as to wave or *saw* backwards and forwards, and even the larger steam-boats are often upset by them. Barnaby described this river so minutely in the course of conversation, that I almost dread encountering its dark and turbid waters. Imagine a stream five thousand miles in length, flowing through all changes of climate; its broadest part being thirty miles across, and its narrowest three. Itf water is described as dark, muddy, and un-wholesome—even the fish it produces are unfit to eat; its banks are desolate and marshy, and the mouth, where it empties itself into the ocean, swarms with alligators.

On all subjects he was, as before stated, ready, and when we spoke of our visit to the Criminal Court he gave us many extraordinary anecdotes relating to cases which had come under his own observation, and amongst them I must preserve one for the gratification of my readers; for I never heard a wilder and more fearful tale than

THE MONOMANIAC.

Although the march of intellect has dissipated many of our nursery superstitions; and those fearful visitations of the dim and shadowy world, which staggered even the wise and learned of by-gone days, have evanesbed into "airy nothings" before the spirit of enquiry and the research of science; yet, in the daily occurrences of life, enough remains of the wild and wonderful, to startle the sceptic and perplex the philosopher.

There could scarcely have been found a finer sample of manhood, than in the person of Harry Elmore, when, at the age of two-and-twenty, with high spirits, an ardent temperament, and a mind cultivated by education and improved by travels, he was recalled from Europe, by the demise of his father, to take possession of an extensive property in South Carolina. The deceased Mr. Elmore, a kind and indulgent master, had earnestly recommended the numerous slaves on his esta-blishment to the protection of his son, who, a native of Carolina, brought up from his childhood on the plantations, had been an especial favourite with all. The last wishes of his father were but in unison with his own, and nowhere in the far South, could be found a happier race of sable mortals than the cultivators of the broad lands of Ranoke.

It was a proud day for one of this motley group when Harry

Elmore returned to the paternal roof. The fine muscular frame of Hector seemed to dilate with importance when recalled from his ordinary employment to immediate and personal attendance upon his young master. His mother had been Harry's nurse, and he bore him all that affection which kindness never fails to produce in the degraded Negro. Some attention, from this circumstance, had been paid to his education; and although his claims to erudition might not have been allowed beyond the sphere of the plantation, he combined, with more than the ordinary shrewdness of his race, other qualifications which were generally acknowledged and appreciated; he could swim like a fish—fight like a tiger—and run like a greyhound! These accomplishments were prized by no one more than his master. A keen sportsman, in a country where the chase is not unattended with danger, Hector's courage and abilities had been, on more than one occasion, called into action; and, to crown all, he was possessed of a virtue, the more valuable on account of its rarity—he was abstemiously sober! It was soon remarked, the new proprietor of Ranoke was not likely to follow in the steps of his predecessor. Satisfied with the fortune he had inherited, he left the management of his affairs to overlookers, and appeared inclined to follow the example of a country where longevity is seldom attained, but by habits diametrically opposed to the high living and profuse hospitality of a Southern planter.

The society of his immediate neighbourhood was a fair sample of the whole State, where precocious manhood promised little but premature old age, and all seemed anxious to crowd into a brief existence, as much of enjoyment as could be obtained by unlimited indulgence in the joys of the race-course and the chase, and the more dangerous excitements of the bottle and the gaming table!

Harry Elmore, although his intellectual attainments rendered him superior to such society, had not escaped its contaminating influence; and whilst his mind had been cultivated by European society, his morals were not improved by an introduction to the sporting circles of England, or his initiation to the "salons" of Paris.

Freed from all salutary restraint or controul, and never having known a mother's affection, who had died in giving birth to her only child, he rushed on a career of dissipation and extravagance, which presaged a speedy shipwreck both of health and fortune: the quiet mansion of his father was now the rendezvous of all the boon companions of his daily sports and nightly orges, and morning too often broke on scenes of disgraceful riot and disgusting inebriety.

In the course of two years, large sums lost at play, and responsibilities incurred for others, made a frightful inroad into a fortune, mor than sufficient for the ordinary indulgencies, or even luxuries of life

On the last day of Charleston races, a horse of Elmore's had won contrary to general expectation; remarks, implying doubts of the fairness of the race, were made by several losers on the occasion, and, in the course of an angry altercation, Colonel Darwin, one of his most intimate friends, received a gross insult from a person betwixt whom aad Elmore a grude of old standing existed; a meeting was appointed for the following morning, and with strong feelings against his opponent, he readily undertook the support of his friend.

In Carolina the office of second is by no means the nominal situation custom, and the amelioration of the sanguinary code of the " duello," has rendered it in Europe ; nor is the meeting a secret, being generally confided to two or three friends, who attend as witnesses or coadjutors, as circumstances may render necessary.

On the following morning, at the usual place for deciding such affairs, a lone part of the sea-beach, commonly designated " The battle ground," the principals were at their post, each attended by two friends, besides the immediate seconds; and from the dark looks, and stern civilities mutually exchanged, it was evident that no amicable arrangement was anticipated.

The first fire was harmless, and the principals advanced one pace by agreement, when a remark from the opposing second gave offence to Elmore, and his reply seemed a pre-concerted signal for a general combat ; pistols were discharged—and then the desperate close and struggle, which rendered the use of the Spanish knife (a weapon constantly worn about the person) available, gave to the conflict the character of a deadly and sanguinary strife !

An alarm was given, and by the time several persons had arrived at the scene of contention, three of the combatants were down, to rise no more ! and Elmore, fainting from loss of blood, and covered with wounds, was barne from the frightful " mèlée," by the timely interposition of Hector !

It was three months before he arose from a bed of sickness, insensibility, and pain ; his medical attendant, Mr. Stanley, an old college friend, watched the progress of his lingering recovery with intense anxiety, and observed, with sorrow and surprise, that improving health brought no elasticity of mind, or the usual joyful anticipations of convalescence ; a gloom was on his brow ; his eye either wild and startling, or settled into the expression of deep and fearful abstraction.

He was shortly enabled to leave his chamber, and however his friends might regret the anguish depicted on his countenance, they rejoiced to find he was a wiser, if a sadder, man. A minute inquiry into his affairs, the immediate dismissal of his principal overlooker, and an entire change in his habits, were the first proofs of a determined reformation ; the sale of many of his valuable horses, and a diminution of his domestic establishment, followed ; his accustomed sports were neglected, his rifle thrown by, and Hector's situation became a sinecure ; who, as if to accommodate himself to " the mode," gradually became as miserable and melancholy as his master.

Time seemed to bring no alleviation to the strange malady which oppressed him ; his meals—his walks—were solitary, and with the exception of Mr. Stanley, he had neither visitor nor companion : it was n vain, in the blended character of friend and physician, he strove to fathom his mind's desease ; to all inquiry and solicitude he was obstinately silent.

A year past away, his health was re-established, but the gloom of his spirit still remained ; and if, at times, his bearing assumed somewhat of the gaiety of former days, it was instantly followed by a corresponding depression.   He had, however, strictly adhered to his plans of economy, and one year's personal attention had done much in repairing the derangement of his affairs.

At this poriod he iuformed Mr. Stanley of his intention of again visiting Europe ; and he spoke of some business of importance still un-arranged, and also expressed a hope that, in change of scene and climate, he might recover his wonted tone of mind, and accustomed spirits.   It was rumoured that he had formed an attachment in England, not entirely obliterated during his brief and desperate crreer ; of this circumstance he made no communication to Stanley, who, however, hoped that his visit might have for its object the renewal of such con-nexion, and lead to a permanent domestic arrangement ; it was evident he anticipated an absence of some years, from the extensive tour he contemplated in Europe.

Everything was prepared for his departure ; on the previous evening, Stanley, who was his guest for the night, having promised to accom-pany him to Charleston, his place of embarkation, was congratulating him on the necessity of a sea voyage.   " You have, no doubt," said Elmore, " thought my conduct both strange and ungrateful, in not communicating to you the cause of my depression, and altered de-meanor ; I had hoped time would have dissipated an illusion, (for illusion it must be !) and rendered unneccssary the confession of a weakness, which must excite yeur pity, if not your contempt !"

" Explain yourself, I beg," replied Stanley.

" You are well aware," continued Elmore, " I am not superstitious ; nay more, that my general scepticism has been the cause of frequent argument between us ; how, then, shall I tell you I am, at this moment, haunted by a spectre ! whose constant visitation is, undermining my health. and destroying my peace ?"

" Good heavens ! can you be serious ?" exclaimed his friend.

" Perfectly so !" proceeded he ; " listen ! if it be a delusion, it is one which has continued for a long year ; alone I have wrestled with it, and have neither yielded to madness nor despair : it is a foe I cannot des-troy, but have, at length, learned to endure.   During my illness, its first impression was as a wild and hateful dream ; it mingled, on my recovery, with my waking thoughts ; its frightful reality increased as my health improved, until it has become a dark shadow and ' plague spot' in my existence !   My nerves have never entirely failed me ; yet even now, when time and habit have accustomed me to its presence, its shadowy influence thrills my very marrow !"

" Where, and at what time," inquired Stanley, " does it most predominate ?"

" At all times, and every where ;" replied he, " even now, 'tis there !" pointing upwards, and gazing wildly on the high and darkened wainscot.

" It's form—*my own dissevered head;* dark drops of gore are falling from it, and the eyes are fixed in the dull and stony glare of death !''

It was night, and Stanley felt the blood creep coldly through his veins, as Elmore, with his eyes fixed on the spot immediately above where he was seated, made this strange disclosure.

" Yes,'' resumed he, " I have reasoned, I have struggled against it, —still 'tis there !'' He arose, and hastily drew the curtain from the window, " and there !'' he cried, " in the dark cloud of night, in the lighted chamber—in the broad face of day—alone—or in the crowd— that cold eye and ghastly head are still before me, but I have not entirely sunk under it,'' rejoined he, " nor will I :—it must be some optical illusion proceeding from my late illness ; time and chanfie of scene may, at length, remove it ; or, at least, render it less distressing. I have thus,'' concluded he, " explained myself, as I wished you to know the real cause of my uneasiness ; but I beg you will consider this communication confidential, for, indifferent as I am to the opinion of the world, I would yet avoid the reputation of a ' ghost seer,' or dreamer.''

The following morning Elmore embarked for Liverpool, taking with him Hector ; and Stanley returned, deeply impressed with the strange communication he had received.

*   *   *   *   *   *

Six years elapsed, the greater portion of which were passed in travel, when Elmore was again domesticated at Ranoke ; he had been fortunate in a judicious marriage, and the addition to his family of two lovely children. The errors of his early career had been repaired, his affairs were prosperous, and no person more generally respected in the State of Carolina. The malady so much affecting his spirits had yielped so far to time and resolution. as to be regarded with little of dread and appre- hension ; although, strange to say, it had never entirely disappeared. This was a secret to all but his friend Stanley, who continued his con- stant visitor ; and he had no cause for regret or anxiety, beyond a cir- cumstance which might appear of trifling importance ; viz. the sudden disappearence of Hector.

He had been sent early in the morning on business to Charleston, and had not returned ; inquiries were made, and it was ascertained he had neither executed his commission, nor been seen in the neighbour- hood. His long attachment to Elmore, and apparent affection for his children, made his absenae a source of great uneasiness ; his steady habits and extreme sobriety, rendered it more extraordinary ; apprehen- sions were naturally entertained for his safety ; and when weeks elapsed, and no tidings of him were received, Elmore feared his worse anticipa- tions had been realized.

It was one of those calm and delightful evenings, nowhere more highly appreciated than in a southern climate, when the extreme heat of day is succeeded by the cool night-breeze, laden with the perfume of the orange-tree and the myrtle, Elmore sat with his family beneath a verandah adjoining the house, and overlooking a landscape of surpassing beauty. His mind was calm and serene; the mental disease he had laboured under was all but subdued—the visitations it produced had become "few and far between;" and as he gazed upon his wife and children, he felt once more a proud and happy man. They remained in conversation until it became nearly dark; the moon arose partially obscured, and they were about retiring, when a servant entered, and announced the return of Hector.

"Tell him to come to me instantly," hastily answered Elmore.

"He must speak with you, sir," he says, "before he enters the house," replied the servant.

"*Must!*" said Elmore. "Well, well; I suppose he is ashamed of his absence, and wishes to give me some explanation. Tell him I'll come to him;" and assuring Mrs. Elmore he would not be long, he passed from the verandah through the apartment to the front of the house.

Mrs. Elmore retired with the children. Lights were brought, and she awaited with some anxiety the return of her husband. Ten minutes —a quarter—half an hour elapsed, and still he did not appear. She at length became uneasy, and rang for the servant; to her inquiry he replied, Mr. Elmore had walked with Hector up the avenue a distance of some fifty yards from the door, and had not returned.

It was now quite dark. She felt alarmed, and hastened to the front of the house; all was silent—she called, but no answer was returned; and she rushed down the steps leading to the avenue, followed by the servants. There was a rising ground about thirty yards from the house, and workmen had been employed during the day felling timber. She had reached the spot, when a wild and piercing shriek broke upon her ear; and the moon at that moment bursting from a dark and heavy cloud, shone full upon the giant form of Hector; he still brandished a large wood-axe, streaming with blood, and at his feet lay the *headless corpse* of Harry Elmore!

CHAPTER VI.

" A fig for those by law protected,
  Liberty's a glorious feast."

BURNS.

I this morning visited the different public institutions on Long Island ; one of them is a lunatic asylum. The building is handsome, and is remarkable for a spacious and elegant staircase ; the wards might, I think, have been cleaner and better ordered. At a short distance from this building is another, called the Almshouse—that is to say, the workhouse of New York. In the same island is the Long Island farm, where young orphans are nursed and bred. I was taken to these institutions by water, in a boat belonging to the Long Island jail, and rowed by a crew of prisoners, who were dressed in a striped uniform of black and buff, in which they looked like faded tigers. They took me by the same conveyance to the jail itself ; it is an old and dreary prison. The prison for the State at Sing-Sing is, on the other hand, a modern jail; that and Mount Auburn are the largest and best examples of the silent system.

There are in New York excellent hospitals and schools, literary institutions and libraries, an admirable fire department (made perfect by constant practice), and charities of every sort and kind. In the suburbs there is a spacious cemetery, unfinished yet, but every day improving. The saddest tomb I saw there was the stranger's grave, dedicated to the different hotels in the city; on a plain white marble slab I read the name of Ellen Gray, and from a friend heard her story, which tells a fearful tale of one of the wild and lawless spirits with which this land of enterprise and liberty has too much abounded.

ELLEN GRAY.

The wisdom of the aged, the sage lessons of experience, the oft repeated and the lengthened homily, how slight are their effects upon the young, the thoughtless, and the gay! Listened to with impatience in moments of anticipated pleasure, and unheeded in the brief career of happiness, sorrow and disappointment alone recal their oft repeated warnings, and, when too late, the poignancy of remorse is blended with the inutility of regret!

Gay summer reigned in the heart of Ellen Gray, and with a restless air she listened to the advice and remonstrance of her only relative, an aged grandmother. The subject of their conversation was, the propriety of an acquaintance which Ellen had recently contracted with one, an entire stranger to her family and connections.

"I am sure Captain Faulkner is a gentleman," warmly replied the sanguine and enamoured girl, in reply to some covertly expressed doubt of her grandmother's, " and as to his being an American, are we not sprung from a common stock? Were he a Spaniard, a Portuguese, or a Frenchman, you might object on the score of nationality."

"It is not that," calmly continued Mrs. Gray, "but no one here knows him, and there is a mystery about him of which I do not approve."

There was a mystery about Captain Faulkner, but that mystery was his strong hold on the heart and imagination of his warm and interesting advocate.

Ellen Gray, deprived in early childhood of both her parents, had been brought up by her grandmother, who resided in a quiet but respectable manner, on a small annuity, at a pleasant village in the vicinity of the busy town of Liverpool.

At some place of public amusement, Captain Faulkner, a young and dashing American, attached, he said, to the naval service of the States, had been introduced to Ellen. He had been at once struck with the beauty and various winning graces of his new acquaintance, openly expressed his admiration on a subsequent interview, and had been, at length, received by Mrs. Gray, although with some misgivings, as a suitor to her interesting but portionless, grandchild.

Ellen's education had been extremely limited, but a great fondness for reading had enabled her to remedy many of its defects. With no one to controul her choice, the library of the village displayed its tempting treasures; the interesting events of history were soon superseded by the charms of poetry, or the mysterious intricacies of the latest novel; and she became, in a short time, deeply initiated in the fashionable and exciting literature of the day, in which the Lovelaces and libertines of former times have been succeeded by the exhibition of remorseless murderers and pirates, arrayed in a false grandeur, and surrounded by all the high qualities of heroism, magnanimity, and gloomy glory.

From such sources Ellen had drawn her heroes; and as she lingered with delight upon the glowing pages of Byron and Scott, was borne in imagination through Seyd's blazing halls by Conrad, or wandering over sunny seas, green islands, and romantic rocks, with the interesting pirate, Cleveland.

Faulkner seemed to her heated fancy the realization of her early visions, and she listened with a willing ear to his adventures. He told her of the wonders of the New World, its boundless prairies, vast rivers, and sea-like lakes, and painted a fairy bower in the far west, adorned with all the charms of Eden!

In such a frame of mind the susceptible heart of Ellen was soon won, and, in a few short weeks from their first acquaintance, she became the wife of the interesting, although somewhat mysterious stranger!

A few months sufficed to dissipate many of her illusions; Faulkner was still kind and attentive, but at times gave way to bursts of raging passion, developed by circumstances as causeless as their effects were extraordinary. His sleep was disturbed by strange phantasies, and all the efforts of the kind, devoted wife, were at times insufficient to calm his wild and fearful perturbations. For hours he would roam with Ellen by the sea beach, and, as the wind and storm ruffled the waters of the ocean, gaze with longing eye upon each gallant ship, until a partial frenzy seemed to possess him; during which, words of strange import burst from his impatient lips, mingled with raving blasphemies, and imprecations on his own devoted head. With none to cheer or comfort her, the hapless Ellen strove, by every endearment, to win the confidence of her wayward husband. She offered to leave her native land, and share with him the dangers of the sea; and it was at length decided, that, in a few weeks, they were to embark for America. Faulkner had never been explicit, either to Ellen or Mrs. Gray, respecting his present means, or future expectations; he had merely stated his family were living on their property in a delightful part of Rhode Island; that he had followed the sea from boyhood, and, after various adventures, attained the command of a vessel, in which he had realised wealth, and gained distinction in many a desperate conflict with the lawless adventurers who roamed the seas of the Western Indies. He had last sailed on board a packet-ship from New York, in which city he stated himself to be well-known, and possessing both influence and connection; curiosity brought him to England, where the charms of Ellen had detained him beyond the period fixed for his return, and some consequences had resulted through his long estrangement from the duties of his profession which he feared might prove injurious to his interests. The latter was the the cause he assigned for his outbreaks of temper and disturbed imagination ; and he found a kind and willing listener to his crude excuses in his young and devoted wife. "Once more on the deck of his good ship," he said, "and he would be all she wished ; and when a few years had enabled him to fulfil the brilliant course he eagerly anticipated, a fairy home in the far west should receive his bride, bright as her young and ardent fancy pictured."

It wanted but a few weeks of their proposed departure ; Ellen had been occupied in preparations, and in earnest requests to her aged relative to accompany them. But all her efforts to conquer the repugnance felt by her grandmother to the object of her choice were vain ; "she hoped, wished, prayed," she said, "for the best ; and that her dear child might never repent the precipitancy of her engagement ; and although deprived of all she loved on earth, trusted she might live to hear of the fulfilment of her sanguine hopes, and increasing happiness." It was evening ; Ellen and her husband were seated in one of the boxes of the Liverpool theatre, in which town they were in temporary lodgings ; the performance had progressed some way, when she observed his brow wore again that peculiar gloom which had so often distressed and alarmed her ; his eye was wild and restless, and he appeared to pay no attention to the play, which had, hitherto, seemed to interest him. On watching his anxious glance towards some object which had evidently attracted his attention, she observed a man of mean appearance, dressed in the garb of a sailor, seated immediately below them in the pit ; his countenance would have been strikingly handsome, but for a complexion burnt almost to negro blackness, and seamed with many a deep, unsightly scar, and wearing an expression blended with ruthlessness and cunning, that told of long companionship with danger and guilt. He was evidently seeking to attract the notice of Faulkner, who appeared to have no anxiety for the recognition ; at length a loud hem ! uttered by stentorian lungs, as he raised himself to his almost giant height during a pause in the performance, could no longer allow him to remain unheeded by her husband ; and with a countenance blanched with apparent terror, and a voice tremulous with ill-suppressed emotion, he begged her to excuse him for a moment, and quitted her side. As he left the box, her eye wandered to the stranger, when she observed a smile of triumph curl his lip, and he slightly touched his hat to her as he withdrew from the seat he had occupied. Ellen waited with considerable anxiety for the return of her husband. The first performance was over—still he came not ; an hour elapsed—her agitation became extreme ; and when she found herself alone, on the fall of the curtain, it amounted to an expression of agony which could not be concealed from those in her immediate vicinity. She arose for the purpose of leaving the house (most of the visitors of which had now departed), and, as she stepped into the lobby, was met by Faulkner ;

OF AMERICA.

53

his appearance was wild and haggard, and he had evidently been drinking ; he made some hurried excuse, and they passed into the street together. The house where they boarded was at some distance, in a lonely and retired street ; as they proceeded on their way, she observed that some person was following them ; and on turning her head, perceived, close behind them, the stranger who had caused her husband's absence ; he passed them, again saluted her, and, in a careless tone, bid Faulkner "not to forget."

On their arrival at home, the latter, after seeing Ellen to her apartment, pleaded an engagement ; and assuring her his stay would be short, despite her tears and entreaties, left her. She threw up the window on his shutting the door, and saw the stranger apparently waiting for him. A loud imprecation burst from the lips of Faulkner, which was lost in the wild laugh of the coarse sailor, who placed his arm within that of his companion. Faulkner lingered for a moment, and gazed anxiously up to the darkened window, from which she immediately withdrew ; a hastily murmured benediction, blended with her name, burst from his lips, and struck like a knell upon the heart of Ellen. They were the last words she ever heard from one she loved, not wisely, but too well !

Days—weeks—passed away, and no information cheered the miserable wife. The proper authorities made every inquiry and search, but no tidings could be obtained of Faulkner or his strange companion. Ellen still lingered in fond expectation, nor, for a length of time, would receive the general opinion entertained,—of his absence being *voluntary ;* and even when time, and a connecting chain of circumstances, almost forced such sad conviction on her, each night, ere she pressed her lonely couch, her prayer was blended with some faint and vague anticipation of his return on the morrow. Months had elapsed since the disappearance of Faulkner, when Ellen's hopes were revived by the return of a packet-ship from New York, which had sailed on the very morning of his departure. A stranger had obtained a passage at the latest moment of her sailing the description of whose person corresponded precisely with her husband's, and the name on the ship's manifest was Faulkner ; he had been communicative with the captain during the voyage, who had also seen him frequently in the city of New York previous to his return. No doubt remained with Ellen that he lived ; and, however strange and mysterious his absence, she framed, in her sanguine imagination, causes which might have prompted it ; and her enduring affection found excuses, and forgiveness of its cruelty. One cause alone prevented her immediate departure for the United States ; the lonely and abandoned wife was about to become a mother ; the timid fears of the woman were overcome by the fond anticipations of the wife, and she hoped with her new claim upon his love, yet to redeem the truant husband in the fond and doating father.

Beneath the happy roof of her childhood, and under the fostering care of her more than parent, Ellen gave birth to a lovely boy ; and as the hour of nature's anguish subsided, she forgot, in the embrace of joy, her bereavement, and her wrongs, while gazing on the miniature resemblance of their still-loved and cherished author. The fatigue and excitement of the last few months, which the more elastic mind and vigorous frame of Ellen, supported by hope, that blessed boon to the wretched, had enabled her to sustain, pressed heavily on the increasing age and infirmities of the kind-hearted Mrs. Gray ; and in a few weeks from the birth of her infant, Ellen stood a pale mourner by her grandmother's death-bed, and closed those eyes, fixed, to the last, in kindness on her; and as the dull cold earth was heaped upon her lonely grave, felt, more than ever, called upon to find a protecter for her child ; a short period sufficed to arrange her affairs ; the little property possessed by her grandmother became her's ; and with her infant child, and a tried and faithful female domestic, she prepared to leave her native land in search of her husband. The vessel in which Ellen embarked for New York was replete with every comfort and accommodation, and her interesting appearance excited the attention and kindness of all on board. Her boy grew in strength and beauty, and, as she held him in her arms on the deck, he seemed to enjoy the rustling breeze ; already the infant incipient sailor bent lovingly to the green waters, and received, without flinching, the rough baptism of the salt dashing spray. A few weeks brought them within sight of their destination ; and with a throbbing pulse, and beating heart, Ellen stepped her foot upon the crowded Battery ; in that moment she almost expected, by one of those vague and indescribable sensations which, at times, rush suddenly to the heart, to be received into the arms of Faulkner : she gazed around, —all was strange ! No welcome voice saluted her ; and again her heart sunk within her, on finding herself a lone stranger on a foreign strand. The kindness of her fellow-passengers relieved her from all trouble in seeking a residence, and, in a few hours, she was comfortably located in a quiet respectable boarding-house. She had some letters of recommendation, but her first inquiries were, of course, for her husband. " Faulkner,—Faulkner," was reiterated to all inquiries— " was he a merchant ?—did he keep a store ?" but on her stating his rank and profession, she was distressed by receiving, on all occasions, a negative to her anxious interrogatories.

On the arrival of Ellen at New York, the prevailing topic of conversation was the recent capture of a pirate ;—one of those remorseless beings to whom no shadow of romance or interest could be attached ; who had borne the black flag undisturbed, for years, over the Gulf of Mexico, the seas of the West Indies, and the capes and lonely harbours of the Island of Cuba ; a man of blood ; a reckless outcast, revelling in scenes of drunkenness, blasphemy, and murder ; indifferent to the shrieks of his defenceless victims slaughtered on the solitary seas : such was Gibbs, at that time in the prison of the State ; adjudged and sentenced, and about to pay with a single life for the indiscriminate slaughter of *four hundred human beings*.

With feelings of horror and disgust Ellen listened to various recitals on this subject of general excitement, in the course of one of which her greedy ear caught the mention of a name connected with the pirate' capture, which again aroused her anxiety and hopes.

" Great praise is due to Captain Faulkner," said the narrator, " for his intrepidity in the affair."

There was, then, a Captain Faulkner, known and recognised by his countrymen! She inquired the particulars, and asked for a description of his person; it agreed exactly with his who solely occupied her thoughts, her hopes, and her wishes. Her husband had frequently narrated his adventures with the lawless beings amongst whom Gibbs stood pre-eminent. He lived! she should again see him! and she pressed her boy wildly in her arms, and told him, in accents choked with burning sobs, that he had still a father! The narrator also informed her that Captain Faulkner had been in England about a year since (the time exactly that her husband had disappeared), and promising instantly to seek an interview with him, left her with an assurance that no means should be left untried to restore her to happiness and peace.

Two days after Ellen had received this intelligence she arose before her accustomed early hour. The morning was unusually fine, and she gladly availed herself of the opportunity of a walk with her infant ; the heat of the weather, even in June, rendering such indulgence fatiguing at a more advanced period of the day. Accompanied by her servant, she strolled leisurely towards the Battery, gazed on the wide waters which separated her from the home of her childhood, and watched with rapture the delight of her boy, who stretched his tiny arms towards the ocean, and shrieked with wild glee, as the numerous white winged barques glided over its calm unruffled surface.

On returning home she encountered various groups of persons, all hastening to some common point, and eagerly discussing a subject of evident importance. As she progressed on her route she found herself literally surrounded by a crowd, and took shelter with her child on the steps of a door immediately in full view of the assembled populace, which now swelled, in the extreme distance, a wild and agitated sea of heads.

" I see them," said one ; " they have left the gaol—they are in the cart; now then," and each pressed forward to obtain a nearer view of some approaching object.

Ellen could not have stirred if she had wished it, and had she been able, a feeling, in which was blended curiosity, horror, and a dread of some impending fate rivetted her to the spot.

The fearful object of attraction came slowly forward—a cart, in which, on a raised platform, stood three men, supported by several others, whose presence appeared necessary for their security; for now loud shouts and imprecations resounded on all sides, and cries of " Which is he ? Which is Gibbs ?—the murderer—the pirate—hanging is too good for such a miscreant," were heard above the loud and universal uproar. The throng around the vehicle made the interference of the police necessary, and for a few moments it became stationary directly opposite the spot chosen by Ellen for her security.

"That's him in the middle," shouted a voice immediately beside her.

Ellen gazed wildly in the direction pointed out by the rough speaker, but the immediate object of attraction had his face averted; the man on his right was a negro, and in his almost sable companion she had no difficulty in recognising the dark and fearful stranger who, in Liverpool, had borne her husband from her arms. A faint sickness overpowered her; she clenched the iron support on which she leant until the blood started from her fingers. The motion of the vehicle changed the position of the third party—his face was turned full towards her, and she saw in the pale and shackled pirate—the blood-stained and remorseless murderer—*her long lost husband!* A wild shriek burst from the hapless Ellen, when a man of gentlemanly deportment rushed forward, and bore her safely from the crowd; directed by her domestic he conveyed her home. Delight was perceptible on the countenances of her expectant friends, amongst whom, awaiting her return, was the person who had promised to seek her husband; for in her conductor he recognised the individual known to him as Captain Faulkner.

No word of explanation came from the pale lips of Ellen; she unclosed her eyes but once, and fixed them on her child. A convulsive shudder—one long drawn sigh—and her gentle spirit passed to a brighter home than even her fondest hopes had ever painted!

＊　　　＊　　　＊　　　＊　　　＊　　　＊

Having made arrangements for securing a passage home in the George Washington, packet ship, which was advertised to sail in June, that being the month in which I had determined, if prevented by no accident in the course of my rambling, to leave America, I left for Boston by water, stopping at Providence or Rhode Island, whence the rest of the journey is made by coach. I stayed but a few hours in the place; Rhode Island is a State of itself, and was once the seat of Government of the celebrated Philip the Indian king, who was one of the latest, firmest opposers of the "white man" in America. Here I saw the little Warden Theatre, the last place that ever witnessed the inimitable acting of George Frederick Cooke. I left in the evening for Boston, and found myself comfortably established in the Tremont House; it is a hotel on the grandest possible scale, has more galleries, colonnades, piazzas, and passages than I can remember or the reader would believe, and is some trifle smaller than Bedford-square. On the following morning, which was Sunday, when I got into the streets, the air was so clear, the houses were so bright and gay, the sign-boards were painted in such gaudy colours, the gilded letters were so very golden, the bricks were so very red, the stone was so very white, the blinds and the area railings were so very green, the knobs and plates upon the street doors so marvellously bright and twinkling, and all so slight and unsubstantial in appearance, that every thoroughfare in the city looked like a scene in a pantomime.

The suburbs are, if possible, even more unsubstantial-looking than the city, the white wooden houses (so white that it makes one wink to look at them) with their green jalousie blinds, are so sprinkled and dropped about in all directions without seeming to have any roots at all in the ground, and the small churches and chapels are so prim and bright and highly varnished, that I almost believed the whole affair could be taken up piecemeal like a child's toy, and crammed into a little box.

The city is a beautiful one, and cannot fail, I should imagine, to impress all strangers very favorably. The private dwellings are for the most part large and elegant, the shops extremely grand, and the public buildings handsome. The State-house is built upon the summit of a hill, which rises gradually first, and afterwards by a steep ascent, almost from the water's edge. In front is a green inclosure, called the common. The site is beautiful, and from the top there is a charming panoramic view of the whole town and neighbourhood. In addition to a variety of commanding offices, it contains two handsome chambers ; in one the House of Representatives of the State hold their meetings, in the other the Senate.

The tone of society in Boston is one of perfect politeness, courtesy, and good breeding ; the ladies are unquestionably very beautiful in face, but there I am compelled to stop. There are in Boston churches and chapels without number, and for all sects and denominations : the only preacher I heard was named Taylor ; I found his chapel down among the shipping, in one of the narrow old water-side streets, with a gay blue flag waving freely from its roof ; in the gallery opposite the pulpit was a little choir of male and female singers, a violoncello and a violin. The preacher already sat in the pulpit, which was raised on pillars, and ornamented behind him with painted drapery of a lively and somewhat theatrical appearance ; he looked a weather-beaten, hard-featured man, of about six or eight and fifty, with deep lines graven as it were into his face, dark hair, and a stern keen eye.

His manner of riveting the attention of his auditors was peculiar. His imagery was all drawn from the sea, and from the incidents of a seaman's life, and was often remarkably good. He spoke to them of " that glorious man Lord Nelson," and of Collingwood, and drew nothing in, as the saying is, by the head and shoulders, but brought it to bear upon his purpose naturally, and with a sharp mind to its effect ; he had an odd way of taking up his great quarto Bible under his arm, and pacing up and down the pulpit with it, looking steadily down, meantime, into the midst of the congregation ; thus when he applied his text to the first assemblage of his hearers, and pictured the wonder of the church at their presumption in forming a congregation amongst themselves, he stopped short with his Bible under his arm, in the manner I have described, and pursued his discourse after this manner.

" Who are these ? who are they ? who are these fellows ? where do they come from ? where are they going to ? Come from ? what's the the answer ?" leaning out of the pulpit, and pointing downward with his right hand, " From below !" starting back again, and looking at the sailors before him, " From below, my brethren ; from under the hatches of sin, battened down above you by the evil one—that's where you come from !"—a walk up and down the pulpit—"and where are you going ?"—stopping abruptly—" where are you going ? Aloft !" very softly, and pointing upwards, " aloft !" louder—" aloft !"—louder still ; " that's where you are going, with a fair wind, all taut and trim, steering direct for heaven in its glory, where there are no storms or foul weather, and where the wicked cease from troubling, and the weary are at rest."

The usual dinner hour in Boston is two o'clock ; a dinner party takes place at five, and at an evening party they seldom supper later than eleven, so that it goes hard but one gets home, even from a rout, by midnight.   There is very little difference between a Boston and a London party, excepting that you are certain to see an unusual amount of poultry upon the table, and at every supper at least two mighty bowls of hot stewed oysters, in any one of which a half-grown Duke of Clarence might be smothered easily.

There are two theatres in Boston of good size and construction, but sadly in want of patronage. The few ladies who resort to them sit, as of right, in the front row of the boxes.

There is no smoking room in any hotel, but the bar is a large room with a stone floor, and there people stand and smoke and spit and lounge about all the evening, dropping in and out as the humour takes them. There, too, the stranger is initiated into the mysteries of gin-sling, cock-tail, sangaree, mint-julep, sherry-cobbler, timber-doodle, eye-opener, holdfast, fog-clearers, and other rare and curious drinks.

Before leaving Boston I devoted one day to an excursion to Lowell. I made acquaintance with an American railroad, on the occasion, for the first time. There are no first and second class carriages as with us ; but there is a gentleman's car and a ladies' car, the main distinction between which is, that in the first everybody smokes, and in the second nobody does. As a black man never travels with a white one, there is also a negro car, which is a great blundering clumsy chest, such as Gulliver put to sea in from the kingdom of Brobdignag. There is a great deal of jolting, a great deal of noise, a great deal of wall, not much window, a locomotive engine, a shriek, and a bill. In the centre of the carriages in winter there is usually a stove fed with charcoal or anthracite coal, which is, for the most part, red hot.

Lowell is celebrated for its factories, all of which are carried on by female workers. I happened to arrive at the first factory just as the dinner hour was over, and the girls were returning to their work ; indeed, the stairs of the mill were thronged with them as I ascended. They were all well dressed, but not, to my thinking, above their condition, for I like to see the humbler classes of society careful of their dress and appearance, and even, if they please, decorated with such little trinkets as come within the compass of their means.

It is said that on the occasion of a visit rom General Jackson to this town, he walked through three miles and a half of these young ladies, all dressed out with parasols and silk stockings. They all seemed to me healthy in appearance, many of them remarkably so, and had the manners and deportment of young women, and not of degraded brutes of burden.

The rooms in which they worked were as well ordered as themselves. In the windows of some there were green plants, which were trained to shade the glass; in all, there was as much fresh air, cleanliness, and comfort, as the nature of the occupation would possibly admit of. They reside in various boarding-houses near at hand. The owners of the mills are particularly careful to allow no persons to enter upon the possession of these houses whose characters have not undergone the most searching and thorough inquiry.

At some distance from the factories, and on the highest and pleasantest ground in the neighbourhood, stands their hospital, or boarding-house for the sick. It is the best house in those parts, and was built by an eminent merchant for his own residence. Their industry and economy may be gathered from the fact that, in July 1841, no fewer than nine hundred and seventy-eight of these girls were depositors in the Lowell Savings' Bank, the amount of whose joint savings was estimated at one hundred thousand dollars, or twenty thousand English pounds.

Three things I will also mention, which are facts, but which will, I have no doubt, startle a large class of my readers.

Firstly, there is a joint-stock piano in a great many of the boarding-houses. Secondly, nearly all these young ladies subscribe to circulating libraries. Thirdly, they have got up amongst themselves a periodical, called " The Lowell Offering," a repository of original articles, written exclusively by females actively employed in the mills, which is duly printed, published, and sold, and whereof I brought away from Lowell four hundred good solid pages, which I have read from beginning to end!

Leaving Boston on the afternoon of Saturday, I proceeded back to Providence, intending to return to New York, and go up the River Hudson to Albany, the capital of the State, previously to visiting Philadelphia and Baltimore. I was detained at the Franklin House for three hours, having missed the boats; and the friend who accompanied us related a circumstance that once occurred to him in the same place.

" I once, in this house," said he, " heard one of the most extraordinary stories ever related; and, strange as it may appear, I know it to be true. We have time on our hands, so listen to the narration, as I heard it, of

THE UGLY BEDFELLOW.

" In the winter of the year 18— I was detained, with many others, at this house by a fall of snow, which, in one night, rendered the roads impassable. A ball, attended by the *élite* of the neighbourhood, had been held there on the evening of the storm, and long before the company thought of retiring, all hope of reaching home, excepting by the town's-people (and that with considerable difficulty), had been abandoned. Every effort was made by the proprietor of the establishment to afford accommodation to the numerous parties necessarily detained. The bedrooms were crowded, sofas and chairs were in great requisition, and the house, for three days and nights, was a scene of unusual bustle and excitement.

" It was on the second evening of our confinement, that a party of five, beside myself, were seated round a blazing fire, endeavouring to wile away the long winter night by relating our adventures, and alluding to scenes of a similar inconvenience.

" Why this is nothing," said a young Virginian, who had been the life of our little party, " to an accident that once occurred to me. Talk of six in a room," continued he, " I'd sleep six deep rather than have the one ugly bedfellow it was my fate, on that occasion, to encounter." Of course, we all expressed anxiety to hear his adventure, and the waiter having replenished the " whiskey jug," and placed an additional log upon the fire, he thus commenced his narration :——

" There are two things," said he, " that we Virginians particularly pride ourselves on. 'Tis true, in corn we cannot equal Kentucky, or, in rice compete with Carolina, but, as regards tobacco and snakes, I calculate we'll not turn our backs on the whole Union ! Their merits need no individual eulogy, as you no doubt are aware we swear by the one in America, and even in Europe they don't hesitate to puff the other.

" I was hunting in the fall of last year with a friend who has a fine estate near Norfolk, when, finding game scarce in our immediate vicinity, he proposed a party to a summer residence he had about twenty miles in the mountains ; servants were sent on some days previous to prepare everything for our reception, and we arrived, a party of ten, on the evening of a cold October night, fully prepared to commence on the morrow our work of slaughter and destruction. We sat down to an excellent supper, and prolonged the night with song and recital of adventure. One of our party had been engaged in the Indian warfare in Florida, and his fearful recitals of scalping and bush-fighting I remember to have had a great effect on my imagination ; we ' kept it up' until a late hour, when, with a flushed cheek, and rather an unsteady step, I found my way to my chamber.

" It was a large room on the ground floor, the windows of which looked over an extensive garden ; a cheerful fire blazed on the hearth, which had been kept up, as I was informed, all day—a necessary precaution considering the lateness of the season. The night was intensely cold, the bed seemed to invite me to a comfortable repose, and was near the fire, by which I quickly undressed, and was, in a few minutes, ' wrapt in measureless content.'

" I must (as I ascertained in the sequel) have been in bed some hours ; I had passed through various changes of the strange fantasies of sleep, when, influenced perhaps by the recitals of my friend from Florida, I thought myself with him engaged in an Indian skirmish ; we were defeated—it was in vain my companion called on me to fly ; my limbs were powerless ; with every inclination to escape, I appeared, by some invisible agency, rivetted to the spot; I was overpowered, alone, and a prisoner ; bound to the stake, I thought I was about to realise some of his descriptions of their ingenuity of torture; a dark and ferocious form seemed twining a burning cord around me, which every exertion I made appeared to tighten ; my left arm was already confined, but I still struggled to keep the fearful shackle from my throat; a suffocating heat pervaded my whole frame, a thick and loathsome vapour choked my articulation, whilst every sense was oppressed and poisoned by a hot and fetid effluvia. My right arm was yet free—with one last effort, I dealt a tremendous blow on the head of my tormentor and —awoke ! That blow had saved my life ! for, with every limb benumbed by the gradual tightening of its infernal coil—its head (which I had st·uck) within a foot of my face—inhaling its rank and overpowering breath—I lay all but powerless in the folds of an enormous ' black snake !' I grasped its throat, and, by an extreme effort, freed my left arm ; with difficulty I managed to reach my knife, and sever the monster.about a foot from the head ; a convulsive struggle, which I felt in every limb, extricated me from its close embrace ; and, deluged with blood, I fainted by the side of my ' Ugly Bedfellow.' "

CHAPTER VII.

"As rolls the river into ocean."
                                        BYRON.

ALTHOUGH America can boast mighty rivers and sea-like lakes, few can vie in varied beauty with the magnificent Hudson, beautiful in all its course, from the dark and wooded mountain where it rises until its junction with a hundred streams at the cascade of Hadley, where the dark rolling Sacondaga, and its silvery stream issue together from their empire in the woods, unite their waters, and quarrel away with angry vehemence, until becoming, as it were, reconciled to their enforced marriage, they jog on quietly together until they mingle at last with that emblem of eternity, the vast, unfathomable, endless ocean, which swallows up the waters of the universe at one mighty gulp. Those who have gazed upon its calm and quiet surface, near the little village of Jessup's Landing, where the river is scarcely a quarter of a mile in width, and seems to sleep between its banks—one of which rises into irregular hills, bounded in the distance by lofty mountains, the other a velvet carpet, just spread above the level of the stream, and running back to the foot of a range of round, full-bosomed hills that are surrounded by a series of rugged cliffs—and have wandered by the numerous little streams, abounding in trout and clear as crystal, meandering through meadows fringed with alders and shrubs of various kinds, wild flowers, and vines, and here and there a copse of lofty trees, will acknowledge few spots in the green earth more picturesque and lovely. Progressing down the stream, which now gradually widens in its course, many a fair island rises from its bosom ; the curling smoke from some farm or cottage, half hid amidst luxuriant trees and foliage, give life and spirit to its quiet loneliness, and on the highland spread their broad shadow on the stream a high and mountainous forest of gloomy pines, destitute of cultivation, except that here and there, at long intervals, the hand of man is indicated by a little clear field, and a rude residence perched like an eagle's nest on some declivity, and again the traveller must confess he never looked upon a scene of more wild and lofty beauty.

It was a lovely day when I gained Albany, and the first person who greeted me on my landing, was my friend the New York theatrical manager, Barnaby Breakspear.

" Come and see our little theatre," said he, and he seized my arm and introduced me to his theatre and his dramatic company.

Actors are sometimes very amusing persons, and there was one amongst Barnaby's company who was a rare treat during my stay at Albany. I was a great deal in " the players' " society, and was highly delighted with this

MODERN PAROLLES.

He was an Englishman by birth, and had come out, with other adventurers, to make his fortune in the theatrical El Dorado! His education, which had been completed somewhere in the vicinity of the New Cut, Lambeth, was not decidedly classical, and his pronunciation slightly at variance with the approved standard of the erudite Walker, although the frequent use of his name in conversation proved, at least, a respect for his authority. Nor were his pretensions to histrionic fame of the most elevated order, his efforts, in the legitimate drama, being principally confined to ruffians, bailiffs, and servants; but, in comic pantomime, terrific combats, or, as the representative of any animal but man, he was unequalled, and was often heard to assert, with energetic gravity, that he considered himself " *The greatest monkey in the United States !*"

Happy was it for the favoured few who, at the little theatre at Albany, could boast the acquaintance of the interesting subject of my present sketch; for, as the merits of each eminent member of the London stage were discussed, he was " Sir Oracle." He knew them all; but his was not that evanescent acquaintance resulting from theatrical connection only. To many of the most eminent he was related! with most of them he had been at school! he had intrigued with all the female performers of doubtful reputation, and narrowly escaped the matrimonial noose with others whose virtue had stood the test of his fascinating solicitations.

It was amusing to hear the easy familiarity with which he spoke of the stars of the theatrical hemisphere! but, unlike most pretenders to intimacy with their superiors, he did not descant on their wealth, their mansions, their equipages, or their festivities, but introduced them at once to the hearts of his admiring audience, as unbending themselves in the congenial atmosphere of the skittle-ground and the tap-room!

At the bar of the tavern next door to the theatre (most American theatres have this convenience, serving as a green-room to the male performers, without trouble or expense to any one but the call-boy), with his hat placed knowingly on one side, to give him more the appearance of Elliston, of whom, personally, he assured his listeners, in his own elegant phraseology, he was "the very spit;" a cigar in his mouth, a black eye—a constant appendage to his pugnacious propensities—and a short thick stick, with which he enforced silence and attention, he was daily in the habit of enlightening a small circle of his especial admirers. I listened to him one morning with peculiar satisfaction; he was, to use his own words, "in great force, getting his steam up;" and as he tossed off his third mint-julep, evidently approximating to "dangerous high-pressure."

"Don't talk to me," said he, "about nine-pins! skittles you mean; never call any thing by its right name; know nothing about the game, either! Go to London—that's the place! Talk of players, poor Charley! he *is* a player!"

"What, Charley Morris?" inquired, with becoming deference, one of his listeners.

"Charley Morris," contemptuously replied he; "Charley Morris be d—d! Who the devil's Charley Morris? I mean my friend Charley, Charley over the water, Charley Kemble! First actor in London in comedy; can't play tragedy. See him in Charles Surface—he *is* a gentleman! Tip 'em all nine—devil of a fellow for skittles!"

"What, you know all the tip-tops?" said one, evidently with the purpose of drawing him out.

"Know 'em! I believe I do," continued he, "you'll see *that*, if any of 'em come to Albany."

"'Tis reported in New York," said another of the party, "that Macready *is* coming!"

"What!" ejaculated our hero, "Bill! Bill Macready? Went to school with him—we're just like brothers. Capital chap, Bill; pleasant tempered fellow—no pride about *him*. Let me see; last time I had a lark with Bill was at Greenwich-fair. You've heard of Greenwich-fair! —held in the park—immense place—half as big as State of New York— hill in the middle, higher than Catskill mountain—everybody goes—all the nobility, King and all—*must go*. Well, *we went*, a snug party. Let's see; there was Dowton, Bill Macready, Charley, *old Charley*, Dick Jones (light-comedy Jones, slovenly Dick we call him), and Dan Terry. Dan always singing, that's a bore, else pleasant fellow Dan; Dowton, jolly old cock, laughing away, never out of temper; there we were—got our pipes—merry as grigs—went in a cart—I drove—the only one steady. Stopped all night, lushing and dancing; next morning—precious mess— ten o'clock rehearsal at Covent-garden—all to be there—got to Waterloo-bridge; you've heard of Waterloo-bridge?—half-a-mile long! —no money to pay the toll—when, just at the nick, who should drive up but Sarah (Charley's sister), Sarah Siddons, the great Lady Macbeth, *going a airing* in her own coach. Charley borrowed half-a-crown—paid the gate; I never shall forget what *a awful shake of the head* she gave Charley. Says she to me—"

Here a loud call for "all the gentlemen savages" (they were rehearsing Perouse) broke the thread of his interesting narration, and I was left in the dark as to the sequel of the adventure.

Albany is a fine city, built on a gentle declivity, rising immediately from the banks of the noble Hudson; the capital, or Senate House, surrounds the whole, and has a very fine appearance. It was originally settled by the Dutch, and most of its houses rejoice in the " gable ends," and other characteristics of the style of building general in Holland. One house particularly attracted my attention; it is built of bricks literally brought from the mother country, and is one of the curiosities of the city; many pine trees give a cool, refreshing shade in summer, and form almost an avenue up the principal street. Near Albany is a settlement of that peculiar people called Shakers, which I visited; but as so much has been already written upon these madmen, I think it unnecessary to enlarge upon the subject here. After a few days stay, I retraced my steps to New York, and from thence went, by boat and railway, to Philadelphia. This is one of the finest cities in the Union, built on a rising ground between the rivers Delaware and Skyulkill. Its only fault, in my opinion, is its regularity; the streets being built at right angles, and nearly reaching from the bank of one river to the other. These main streets are numbered, first street, second street, and so on till about fifteenth street; a large and excellent market in the very centre of them; and the streets that cross them are all named after trees, such as Walnut-street, Chesnut-street, the latter of which is the Bond-street of the Quaker city. All the houses have white dazzling marble steps, and very bright knobs and knockers, and bear a strong family likeness. The Bank, and Mint, and other public buildings are all of pure white marble; a quarry of it is found within a few miles of the city. I visited the site of Penn's treaty with the Indians—familiar to all Englishmen from West's celebrated picture. A handsome stone pillar marks the spot, which is singularly picturesque and beautiful. That the regularity of Philadelphia is tiresome and monstrous there can be no doubt, and so my friend Wilson found it, and more than that, as will be seen in his story of

THE EVILS OF REGULARITY.

" Don't tell me," said Andrew Wilson to his friend Burton, who had been warmly defending the eccentricities of genius, " talent of the highest grade, without regularity, will be eventually outstripped by mediocre attainments, if blended with that powerful auxiliary only."

It was in vain his friend instanced the numerous claimants to the last-mentioned quality, who had left a bright name to posterity, without possessing one particle of the latter. Andrew Wilson was more than his match in discussing so favourite a topic; he had the universe on one side; the tides and the seasons were arranged in his favour; and even the planets, in their regularity of rotation, shone bright upon his argument. Conquered, but not convinced, Burton resigned the friendly contention.

Regularity was, with Andrew Wilson, the first of virtues; his whole conduct was strictly governed by its rules; his sleeping and waking had become, from habit, subservient to its controul; and even his appetite came obedient only at the customary summons to its gratification.

"Well," resumed the more lively and unstable Burton, "I still insist that all extremes carry with them some absurdity, and there may be evils even in regularity; but I give you joy of your proposed American trip, for the city of your destination is a splendid sample of your theory and practice. Philadelphia is built with regularity, its citizens are the most regular in their habits in the States, and erratic or eccentric as the conduct of individuals may be, every one, at least, 'walks in the straight path,' who treads the uniform pavé of the Quaker-city."

A tedious and unusually lengthened voyage (during which the regular habits of Andrew Wilson were much deranged) at last terminated by his safe arrival in America, and about the meridian of a bright day in June, he set foot, for the first time, in the great capital of Pennsylvania.

As the peculiar arrangement of the streets and buildings of Philadelphia may not be known to many of my readers, and although admirably desirable for all purposes of convenience to their resident inhabitants, are still not a little perplexing to strangers; and as my story has reference to that peculiarity, 'tis necessary I should give some account of the plan so judiciously adopted by its original projectors.

No situation could have been more admirably chosen for all the necessities of a large and populous city than the site of Philadelphia. Its wide and open streets rising from the banks of the Delaware, and running in direct lines almost to the parallel waters of the Skyulkill, render it perhaps one of the most cleanly and salubrious locations in the Union. The extensive market intersecting its very centre, and to which access from all quarters, by the peculiar arrangement of the streets, can be immediately obtained, invests it with every possible convenience; whilst the plan of its founders, which was regularity in building, throws around it a quiet charm of order and uniformity, powerfully contrasted with London and most of the continental cities.

The upper part of the three principal avenues leading from the Delaware to the Skyulkill, viz., Walnut, Chesnut, and Arch streets, are, however, to strangers, so much alike as to occasion, at times, much difficulty and embarrassment; and as the streets crossing them at direct lines from first to thirteenth (the number completed at the period of my story), all bear a strong family likeness, they add considerably to the bewilderment of the uninitiated; whilst the polished door handles, the pure white marble steps, the houses uniform and partially alike, with the circumstance that Walnut, Chesnut, and Arch streets have each a theatre, all three of which are on the same side of the way, and nearly parallel with each other, each approachable by marble steps, adorned with columns, statues, and other embellishments, different 'tis true, but yet bearing considerable resemblance to each other, render a guide at times as necessary in the regularity of Philadelphia, as in the arcades and passages of the Rues Richelieu and Vivienne, in the French capital or through the more difficult intricacies of the courts and tortuous windings of the island city.

With feelings of delight Andrew Wilson, escorted by a loquacious porter, walked from the wharf through the lower part of the city, on his way to a quiet boarding house in Eighth-street, kept by a country-woman, to whom he had been recommended in his native city, Edinburgh. It was the Sabbath, and the hour of public worship; the quiet and sunny streets were almost deserted; he gazed delighted on the pure white marble front of the bank, and the various public buildings pointed out with pride by his attendant, and at once saw and appreciated the regularity everywhere observable.

It was late in the evening of his arrival that Andrew Wilson, having made his toilet, proceeded to visit a friend and countryman, who resided in the immediate vicinity of his boarding house. Mrs. M'Kenzie, the landlady of the domicile honoured by his temporary location, pointing out to him with great ease the various bearings of the vicinity, assured him that she would herself await his return; and he departed perfectly satisfied that the regular arrangement of the streets would enable him to steer his course without either difficulty or inquiry. He gained his destination, and felt satisfied that his eulogiums on the Quaker city, were perfectly justified by the favourable results of his first peregrination.

His friend met him with that warmth of feeling and hospitality which, on all occasions, characterises the re-union of long-sundered compatriots on a foreign strand, and the firm grasp and lengthened shake of hands, the eager and mutual inquiry was followed by the oft-repeated pledge in the brimming glass, which welcomed Andrew Wilson "to the home of the brave and the land of the free." Many a tale of former times and pleasant reminiscence connected with " Auld Reekie," beguiled the swift passing hours, and it was late before Andrew Wilson prepared to leave the hospitable domicile of his friend.

" You'll ken your way, Andrew?" said his host.

" Perfectly, decidedly," replied Andrew, and with a hearty farewell, and promise of an early visit on the morrow, he stepped out into the quiet and lonely street.

The cool night air blew freshly upon Andrew Wilson, but had no reviving influence upon his memory: whether the parting glass of toddy had been unusually strong, or the excitement of the late anecdote of his companion produced a partial confusion in his ideas, I know not; it is certain that the designation of the street where he lodged was the only guide his memory could muster. Every Mac but M'Kenzie was upon his tongue, and every number but the right one, came readily to his call. Eighth-street appeared to have expanded in width, and become interminable in its duration; numberless were the white steps he mounted; bells and knockers which he essayed; but not one of the various aroused denizens would recognise the lost and bewildered stranger!

Now Andrew suddenly recollected that in his progress to the house of his friend, he had passed a handsome building, which bore all the outward appearance of a theatre; he retraced his steps, and found himself again before it. There were the marble steps, pillars, and statues which had previously attracted his attention, and he imagined he had at length gained a clue to the labyrinth. The avenue was crossed by Eighth-street, and near the corner on the right hand stood the house he had started from; he looked around, thought he was correct, and, with a feeling amounting to certainty, pulled a bell, he was almost sure he recognized. Twice he essayed the bell but without effect; at length, on his third summons, he was answered by the gruff voice of a man from the upper window, who, with anything but common politeness, desired him to "be off about his business." He now requested the aid of a watchman, who had been regarding him for some time with suspicion, and informed him, as well as he could, the situation of his lodging; it was, he said, in Eighth-street, near the end of an avenue, in which stood the theatre.

"Which theatre?" demanded the guardian of the night; and, with feelings of horror, Andrew learnt that there were three, all much alike, and standing in similar situations! A small gratuity afforded him a guide to each of them, in the person of his informant, but, on examination, he failed to identify the one which was to serve him as a land-mark.

It was now considerably past midnight; the taverns were shut; the streets silent and deserted; and the fatigued and disheartened Andrew began seriously to meditate some outrage by which he might obtain a lodging at the States' charge; previous to which, he, however, determined to make one more desperate effort, and find, if possible, the residence of his friend; and, in so doing, became still further involved, a "lost man" in the intricate regularities of the Quaker-city.

At length, completely worn out, exhausted, and unknowing where he was, in a fit of despair he seated himself upon the step of a doorway, and resigning himself to his fate was, in a few minutes, fast asleep. In dreams he was transported to Edinburgh, and thought himself again engaged in his favorite argument with his friend Burton—when he awoke, wet to the skin from the effects of a sudden pelting shower! He gazed up wishfully at the windows of the house, on the step of which he had been seated; a faint light was perceptible—he was in a civilized city—some one might be up in the house; and if it had been an Indian wigwam, he felt, at the moment, that despite the fear of tomahawk and hatchet, he should knock and demand a shelter: he rang a bell, and shook the door with a feeling of desperation; it opened instantly, and—*Mrs. M'Kenzie—his landlady*, stood before him!

"Eh, sir!" exclaimed the weary watcher, "a dreary time I've had waiting for you, Mr. Wilson; and a beseeming hour in the morning this to be keeping up a lone woman; I guess you have been in proper company."

Poor Andrew offered every apology and explanation, and as he would never allow the whisky-toddy had anything to do with producing the embarrassments of his night's adventure, he was fain to confess that Burton was right, and there came *evils even in regularity !*

*   *   *   *   *   *

I soon became tired of the dullness of the Quaker city, and proceeded to Baltimore, travelling by boat. Now I began to perceive some of the beauties of slavery, as Baltimore is the capital of Maryland, which every body knows is a slave state. Here, as Mathews said in his entertainment, " a man can do what he likes with his own nigger."

Baltimore is a very fine city, and more like London than any other place in America. Here there are high and low, the plebeian and the patrician. The rich planter and merchant and the petty shopkeeper do not jumble together as elsewhere. Here the term Yankee is held in contempt. It has been generally understood in Europe that Yankee is the general denomination of an American, but it is not so ; the Yankee is the down-east man—the trafficking pedlar, and they are looked upon by the Southerners something as we look upon a " Yorkshire bite"—a knowing, trading, cheating set, that will have your head off in no time, " that is, if it's not properly screwed on !"

" Here," said a friend of mine, " is the shop," stopping before a good looking assortment of boots and shoes, with the name of Mowitt over the door; " the story connected with its present proprietor is perhaps one of the most extraordinary on record. The parties have but lately settled here from New York. Just glance at the female behind the counter."

I did so, and saw a very good looking woman, still on the safe side of thirty.

" What is there so extraordinary about her ?" asked I.

" I'll tell you," replied my friend, " That woman has done what few females have ; namely, sat as a juryman on the body of her own husband."

" Nonsense," I replied.

" Nonsense it may be," replied he, " but it is true ; and when we get home I'll read you the story from an official document."

We walked onward, and he then pointed to me a curious looking house, the windows of which were barred with iron, and the whole place surmounted with a high wall.

" What is this," said I ; " a prison ?"

" No," replied he, " 'tis a slave store."

" A slave store !" I answered, and I felt my blood freeze in my veins.

" Yes," answered he ; " here are kept a quantity of human beings, chained up like dogs, and every night blood-hounds are turned into the yard to prevent any of the poor wretches attempting to escape."

" And this," I exclaimed, " is the land of freedom !"

" The Americans are proud of their independence," said he, " and think it so good a thing that they keep it all to themselves ; they don't allow even freedom of speech to a stranger ; you will see the advertise-

ment of the proprietor of this den in all the public papers in Baltimore;
and if you want a nigger you now know where to apply."

I turned with sickening disgust from the foul house of shame, and
returned to Barnam's excellent hotel, where after a repast that would
have satisfied a London alderman, my friend first satisfied me of the
truth of his statement, as regarded the public advertisements for slaves,
and then produced a paper, published in New York, which contained
the account he referred to as regarded the proprietor of the shoe shop.

"Married on Tuesday, by the Rev. William Ash, Thomas Mowitt to
Charlotte Conroy, both of this city."

"The above marriage took place in New York on last Tuesday week,
and thereby hangs a tale of the marvellous. Mr. Mowitt is a respectable boss shoemaker, who keeps several men employed, and amongst
the rest was John Pelsing, who had ingratiated himself so much in his
favour by his faithfulness, industry, and sobriety, that he took him into
partnership about three years since, and had no cause to regret his
kindness. From that period Mr. Mowitt and Mr. Pelsing were constant friends and companions, and boarded in the same house, until
about twelve months since, when one day they were subpœnaed for a
coroner's inquest, which was about to be held on the body of a man that
had been taken out of the Maiden Land Dock. The deceased had all
the appearance of having been a regular dock loafer, and it was the
opinion of all present that he had fallen into the slip while in a state of
intoxication; but the verdict, which was given in a few minutes, was
merely, 'Found drowned.'

"The jury being dismissed, Mr. Mowitt turned round to look for his
friend and fellow-juror, who had been at his side till that moment, but
he was gone; and he thought he saw him running at almost full speed
up Maiden Lane. This struck him as being curious; and it also re-
minded him of another curious fact (at least curious as taken in con-
nexion with his sudden flight), namely, that when Mr. Pelsing had first
glanced at the face of the corpse, he started and turned deadly pale.
Mr. Mowitt then proceeded to his boarding-house, and thence to his
store, to look for his partner, but he was to be found at neither; nor
did he return that night; nor the next day; nor the next; and two
months passed away without bringing any intelligence of him, during
which time Mr. Mowitt had fully made up his mind that there was
some mysterious connexion between his friend and the man that was
found drowned, and that, in consequence thereof, Mr. Pelsing had in
all probability, made away with himself.

Well, so matters rested until a certain day in last June, when a lady
called at Mr. Mowitt's store, and asked for Mr, Pelsing. She was told
the particulars of his story.

"And hasn't he been here since?" she inquired.

"Not since," replied Mr. Mowitt.

"I know he has," said the lady.

"He has not, I assure you, at least, to my knowledge," answered Mr.
Mowitt.

" But I am positive," said the lady, somewhat smartish.

" What proof have you of it ?" inquired the shoemaker.

" The best in the world," returned the stranger, " for I am here, and I and Mr. Pelsing are one and the same person."

And, strange as it may appear, such was the actual fact. Well, the question was, whether Mr. Pelsing was a gentleman or a lady, and it turned out that she was a lady; and, more than that, her name wasn't John Pelsing at all, but Charlotte Conroy; and, furthermore, that she was the widow of the man that had been found drowned. She then stated that her husband was a shoemaker in Philadelphia, to whom she had been married about two years, and who treated her very badly, the consequence of which was, that she picked up his trade by stealth, and when she thought she was sufficiently perfect, equipped herself in men's clothes, and ran off to this city to be the more safely out of the reach of her lord and master. Here, as we have seen, she got into the employment and remained in the confidence of Mr. Mowitt until the time of the coroner's inquest; immediately after which she proceeded to Philadelphia, where she learned that her husband (who had become a wandering loafer) had, on the hint of some friend, set out to New York about a week before, to look for her; but where, instead of an injured wife, he found a watery grave. The upshot of this romantic affair was, that Mr. Mowitt requested Mrs. Conroy to make his house her home; that, after a while, he found that he liked her yet better as Mrs. Conroy than as Mr. Pelsing; that, by virtue thereof, he proposed a renewal of their terms of partnership, which was accepted; that on last Tuesday week Mr. Mowitt and the late Mr. John Pelsing became husband and wife."

he accommodation at Barnam's hotel are the very best in the States; the bedrooms are carpeted, and the bedsteads are *absolutely curtained!* From the proprietor, a very gentlemanly man, and who bears a strong likeness to the immortal Washington, I heard the following account of a scene that passed in the very bedroom I occupied :—

A SCENE AT BALTIMORE;

or, a Passage in the Life of Mr. Peter Watson.

Although the facility of intercourse with the United States has partially obliterated the mutual prejudices which existed between the mother country and her transatlantic offspring, some few years since there were not wanting persons, who, from ignorance or wilful misrepresentations, were induced to consider a sojourn in America as replete with difficulties, and attended with circumstances of great personal risk and inconvenience. Those who have dined in New York at Niblot's, or domiciled at Baltimore with Barnam, will scarcely credit that there have been individuals who, from some strange idiosyncracy or other, have cherished a profane doubt as to the dressing of viands at all at the latter place, or the use of the necessary and convenient instruments of their consumption in the other.

One of this unhappy class was the person, a passage in whose life it is my present business to narrate. Born in that dusky emporium of trade, Birmingham, his travels had hitherto been confined to periodical journeys to London and Manchester, for the purposes of business ; and it was with feelings, almost amounting to horror, he received a proposal from his employers to cross the seas, and visit the far off clime of America. But the spirit of gain was strong within him ; for, however deficient in literary attainments, his commercial education had not been neglected, and few young men of his age could boast a more profound knowledge of the mysteries of pounds, shillings, and pence, than Mr. Peter Watson, of the firm of Bolton and Shorts, of Birmingham. Nor was he wanting in the usual accomplishments of the young aspirants of fashion of his own grade. He dressed well, smoked cigars, played billiards, and doted on the theatre ; and many a bright eye was dimmed when the news was generally promulgated, that the gay Mr. Peter Watson was about embarking for America !

Previous to his departure, he seized every opportunity of acquainting himself with the manners and habits of the country of his destination, in which he was materially assisted by a young friend, whose maternal uncle had been engaged in the " old American war," and whose adventures were admirably calculated to afford him every necessary information ; this advantage, blended with a little light reading in the history of the Buccaneers, and the lives of Captain Kidd, and other worthies of his caste, rendered him, in his own opinion, perfectly conversant with the " lights and shadows" of American life.

I shall not descant on his adventures on ship-board, further than stating, that he was accompanied by three young Americans, returning from the tour of Europe, to whom he proved an excellent relief to the ennui and confinement of the voyage. Like most ignorant persons, he was sheathed in the impenetrable mail of conceit and self-sufficiency ; disbelieving everything he did not understand, tenacious of being imposed on to the extreme, and rudely knowing without possessing a particle of even worldly wisdom, he yet greedily imbibed the most egregious absurdities, so long as they tallied with his own conceptions, or the information he had derived from the sources previously mentioned.

At New York he felt tolerably secure, and confessed that the march of intellect had done much in the way of civilization, since his friend's maternal uncle was engaged in the ' old American war.' He embarked in the steam-boat for Philadelphia with some misgivings, for he remembered a picture which graced the dining-room of one of his employers, representing a quaker gentleman surrounded by some fierce-looking Indians, which had some reference to the city he was approching ; and as the boat neared the quay, he was observed to pass his hand cautiously round his head, and fasten his travelling-cap with particular attention.

Leaving the quiet capital of Pennsylvania with regret, he prepared to proceed in a southerly direction ; as yet he had encountered neither scalping-knife nor tomahawk ; he had wandered on the verdant banks of the Skuylkill without being chased by bear or panther, and been borne on the quiet bosom of the Delaware, whose silvery depths revealed neither sword-fish nor alligator.

But now it seemed fated that his troubles should commence; for he had scarcely set his foot on the steamer which was to convey him to Baltimore, than he found himself surrounded by a dark band of the ' wild forest children,' of whom he had heard such fearful relation (they were a party of peculiarly inoffensive Indians, on their way to Washington, on business with the Congress) arrayed in their native costume; to him danger seemed to threaten in every wave of their feather head-dress, and murder lurk in the gay folds of each scarlet blanket; until now he had been getting rather sceptical as to many of his former anxieties, but they returned with redoubled force; he was amidst a band of veritable Indians, and he had no doubt all the monstrosities of his imagination would follow; and when his ear caught part of a conversation in which " the black population of Baltimore " was mentioned, in conjunction with some wonderful monkey, he recollected his fellow-voyager's description of a people in the far west, who were half horse and half alligator; and, with a trembling misgiving, feared he was about to encounter a southern mixture, equally strange and incongruous in their appearance.

It was late when he arrived in Baltimore, and took up his quarters at Barnham's excellent hotel; fatigued with his voyage, he desired so be shown to his bed-room; the servant conducted him into a large apartment containing two beds immediately opposite each other.

" Does any person sleep in that bed ?" said he, with some anxiety.

" Yes, sir," replied the sable attendant; " sorry we have no single room—quite full to night—very nice quiet gentleman—from England, sir."

Satisfied wth the assurance that a countryman was to be his companion he undressed, and in a few minutes was asleep. And there, for the present, I must leave him.

It was the dramatic season in Baltimore, and the Holiday-street Theatre was nightly crowded to witness the extraordinary performance of an " artiste" who had filled England with his fame, by his faithful delineation of the interesting and arduous character of a monkey; indeed, so natural was each action and grimace, that more than individual doubts were raised as to the " genus " of this wonderful performer. Some insisting that, in reality, he was a veritable baboon, " acting a man;" which, if true, would have considerably depreciated his histrionic talent !

It was a cold night, and the " artiste," who laboured under considerable indisposition, was advised by a medical man in attendance, on no account to remove his dress, which was saturated with perspiration, the effects of great exertion, until he reached home: he promised compliance; but whether he had mistaken the advice of the Esculapius, in imbibing the contents of a jug of strong brandy-and-water which he had prescribed for himself, or thought it better for additional security to be all of a-piece, I am not aware; but, at any rate, he kept on both wig and paint; in which state, wrapped in his cloak, he proceeded to occupy his share of the double-bedded room already tenanted by the recumbent form of Mr. Peter Watson.

He reached his destination in safety; it was late—all was quiet; wearied with exertion, and partially overpowered by the strength of his potation, and some vague idea floating in his brain of a prohibition as to the removal of his dress, he extinguished the light; in all his fearful paraphernalia threw himself on the outside of the bed, and was soon in a happy state of oblivion.

Our traveller slept long and heavily, nor awoke until the breakfast-bell rung through the long galleries leading to the various dormitories. He unclosed his eyes, and fixed them at once on the opposite bed!—A cold perspiration bedewed his face, and his whole frame shook with the intensity of terror, as they encountered the ghastly form of the slumbering "artiste!" Alarm kept him silent; the fearful object snored audibly—was it one of the fierce band he had accompanied from Phila-delphia? or some dreadful native species alluded to in the conversation he had overheard? Could he escape? He dressed himself hastily, and with stealthy steps prepared to leave the apartment, when the bell in the adjoining room rung loudly, which started the monster from his repose, and, at the same instant, brought a servant to the door.

"Bring me a glass of cold brandy-and-water," exclaimed a horrid and unearthly voice, proceeding from the object of his disgust and terror; this was to much for endurance; rushing wildly past the bed, he threw down the astonished waiter, over whom he precipitated himself into the passage, and, in a few hours, perfectly satisfied with the extent of his travels, he was on his way back to Philadelphia.

The minor houses of entertainment, such as are resorted to for oyster suppers, &c., where you can have in great perfection the land crab, a delicious dish, and terrapin soup, also a luxury of the first order, which has only one thing against it, namely, its appearance; its colour being quite black, and the substantial parts of the dish being not unlike, as my friend unfortunately hinted to me at my third spoon-full, negroes toes! an unfortunate remark which made me decline any further acquaintance with it, and indeed *regret* the intimacy which had already taken place between us.

These cellars are often inundated, and a case of the kind occurred during my stay at Baltimore. I was much amused at the conduct of a couple of English tars, who were booming along Front-street, but making a very crooked wake, they stopped in front of a store, where a couple of men were engaged in pumping water out of the cellar.

"Hollo, Tom!" said one, "just look there."

"Why what's that?" replied Tom.

"My eyes, Tom," exclaimed his companion, "if Baltimore hasn't sprung a leak, and they're a pumping her out."

Here is an excellent theatre, at which Booth, who once made such a stir in conjunction with "the Kean" was acting; he has a farm near

Baltimore, and I'm told often kills a pig in the morning, sells it at the market of Baltimore in the afternoon, and enacts *Richard* at night.

The following is related as having occurred to him at Baltimore, and I give it in the shape it was told to me.

A SUIT OF SABLES.

"Your massa and General Jackson bery much alike, Sib!"—re·marked, to his countryman and companion, a male species of that interesting race, the amelioration of whose condition England considered cheap at the outlay of twenty millions sterling;—"Bery much, Cato," replied the intellectual Sib, "more 'specially massa!"

There was a beautiful mystery in the reply that at once pleased and perplexed me; it implied a problem more difficult than Euclid ever proposed, bewildering as eternity, and measureless as space!

That Sib was a philosopher, and that some deep meaning lurked in his qualified assent to Cato's proposition, I had no doubt; but the finishing polish had been communicated to the boots he was employed in cleaning, and a loud call for his attendance removed him hastily from the vicinity of the window, from which I had hoped to hear some solution to his enigma.

Sib was the personal property of an actor as celebrated for his talent and genius as unfortunate in an eccentricity of character, which bordered closely on mental aberration; his was a servitude of affection, for he idolized his master, of whom he was wont to remark, in phrase intended as the perfection of compliment, "that, though possessing a white skin, he had a black heart!"—and when the accident occurred I am about to relate, no individual sympathy was more powerfully developed.

"Ten minutes, gentle*men*," dwelling long and musically on the final syllable of the last word, cried the call-boy of the Baltimore theatre—a signal for expedition in the application of yellow ochre to the heels, and vermilion to the cheeks, to the gentlemen occupying the dressing-rooms of that establishment; where, on the evening in question, 'two Stars kept motion in one sphere;' to witness whose efforts in *Othello* and *Iago*, the house had been crowded at an early hour with the beauty and fashion of that aristocratic city.

But a disappointment not in the slightest degree anticipated, and which proved fatal to the hopes of the audience, and distressing to the manager's (pecuniary) feelings, was about to take place, which was no less than the absence of the Othello of the evening; the orchestra repeated an overture; scouts had been sent in all directions, but still he came not!—and, at length, sickened with 'hope deferred,' amidst a shower of orange-peel, the manager solicited the indulgence of his generous benefactors in behalf of Mr. Jenkins, who had, in the kindest manner, undertaken the part at a moment's notice.

Having quieted the storm in the theatre, he gave way to the one raging in his own bosom; and, burning with indignation, hastened to the residence of the delinquent tragedian, in a humour to brook no denial ; it was in vain Sib remonstrated with him on the impropriety of disturbing his master, who, he assured him, was in bed ; thundering at the door, he demanded admittance ; no answer was returned.   Aroused to a momentary fury, with a powerful effort he burst it open; and there before a large looking-glass, round which were ranged twelve wax candles, their glaring light aided by a blazing fire, in full theatrical paraphernalia, with a visage black as night, stood the object of his search !—

"Most potent, grave, and reverend signiors ; my very noble and approved good masters,"—commenced the actor —the mystery was solved at once ; "the moon had come too near the earth," and his sovereign reason was "like sweet bells, jangled all and out of tune !"

The anger of the manager vanished before the feelings of the man, and humouring his fantasy for some time, he contrived to send for assistance.

His medical adviser [arrived ; his dress was removed, when it was discovered, that not only was his face darkeened for the part, but, by some means, he had communicated the sable tints to his whole body ! —which could not, in his present state, be removed without danger ; a violent illness followed, during which, although communicative on all other subjects, he gave no reason for his adoption of this strange and unusual "suit of sables."

Of the various opinions given on the subject, Sib's was the most amusing ; finding, on the second day, that his master (to whom a powerful opiate had been administered) still bore the appearance of the dusky Moor, he entertained not the slightest doubt that a veritable change had taken place ; and although, in his unbounded affection, he had complimented him on the possession of a "negro's heart," he had sense enough to know that a correspondent colour, as regarded his outward man, would not tend to his personal gratification, or professional advantage ; and therefore considered the transformation as a heavy and palpable judgment. "All comes," said he, "of mocking de colored people ; I neber 'proved of it, by Gole ; massa acts Othello once too much ; he acts himself black at last."

Nor was Sib's opinion removed, until returning convalescence called him to assist in the operation of washing the Blackamoor white.

I dined to-day with a captain of one of the New York packet ships. He was a man of great information, and related many instances of peril and danger which he had met with in crossing the vast Atlantic. Amongst other things he told me of the loss of the Albion, from Liverpool, many years since.

"Was not every soul lost on board of her ?" inquired one of the party.

"All but one," answered he, "and his escape was indeed a miracle."

All begged to hear the particulars, and we listened with breathless attention to his story of the

SOLE SAVED.

It was a bright morning in June, and all was bustle and excitement on the crowded deck of the Albion—a vessel of the first class of packet-ships from the port of Liverpool, bound on her maiden voyage to America—various were the speculations formed upon her probable speed of sailing, and friendly bets were made upon the period of her return, when, amidst the expressed solicitudes of her owners, and the accustomed cheering adieus of parties interested in her living freight, she spread her white wings to the favouring breeze, and was soon but a faint speck in the distant horizon.

Although many, and their fortunes, were borne from the shores of England in that fated bark, but one returned to narrate her strange and fearful story ; of whom 'tis here necessary I should give some particular account.

Jasper Hamilton was the second son of an English baronet, and had been in boyhood the pet child of a doating mother (years since laid in her grave), but who had lived long enough to regret the effects of blind indulgence on her wild and wayward child. She had, with her latest breath, consigned her favourite boy to the consideration and forbearance of her husband, a stern and unrelenting man, on whose latter virtue the capricious and headstrong temper of Jasper had already made fearful inroads.

His elder brother was, in person, slightly deformed ; but possessing a vigorous mind, and intellectual capacity of the highest order ; like many persons labouring under bodily infirmity, his views of ambition and desire of aggrandizement were neither restrained by checks, which nature seemed to have opposed to their fulfilment, nor restricted as to the means by which they might be consummated.

A career of extravagance and dissipation had, at length, estranged Sir Edgar Hamilton from his younger son, when his indignation was aroused by a report that Jasper had committed a sin, the most flagrant in his estimation, viz. that of marriage with a beautiful but portionless girl ; he lost no time in ascertaining the truth of such statement, and on its being proved and substantiated, the parental malediction was hurled upon the newly wedded pair, and Jasper Hamilton was formally disinherited. His latest offence, however, became his safeguard and redemption ; for, in his young wife, he possessed a talisman and treasure : his vicious pursuits were abandoned, and he learned to appreciate the quiet joys of home ; but all his applications to his father were unheeded, and, but for his brother, he would have known all the miseries and privations that attend on poverty and want ; at length, unable to endure the degradation of dependence even upon him, he accepted a mercantile situation in an American house, obtained by his brother's interest, and left his young wife to his protection, until improving fortune should either enable him to send for her, or his father should recal him to his forgiveness ; which his brother promised him it should be his unwearied effort to obtain, and which, he assured him, would be expedited by his temporary expatriation.

Aware of the deep and numerous causes of offence he had given, and oppressed, and partially humiliated, by poverty, he gladly listened to hopes thus held out to him; and, depending on his brother's tried affection and kindness, he left his native land and his young wife, for a temporary sojourn in America, with every hope that fortune might shortly re-unite them under happier auspices.

The Albion made her way with favourable winds towards her destination, and on the fourteenth day after her sailing from Liverpool, had accomplished one-half of her voyage. Night was approaching, dark and gloomy; and as Jasper Hamilton paced the deck late in the evening of that eventful day, his thoughts were of home, and her he had left behind him; and none but those who have experienced such a situation can feel its poignant bitterness. A thousand times he regretted that he had not sought the paternal roof, and, in a personal interview, entreated forgiveness of his father. He thought of his wife, of her lonely desolation, and her beauty, exposed to insult and to injury, and strange misgivings crossed his mind, which had never previously occupied his imagination: he would, in that moment, have given worlds to stand, even a beggar, in his miserable home; and cursed the chance which, in an unguarded moment, drove him from its humble shelter. A slight and drizzling rain now forced him from the deck, and he sought his couch as a relief from misery and thought.

Sleep came, at last, to his fevered brow and throbbing pulse; but, in his dreams, he was again tormented; he thought he saw his father dying—that he called upon his name—but by no effort could he reach him; and his brother stood by, and seemed to mock his agony; suddenly the apartment appeared to whirl around him; a bursting shock, like thunder, struck upon his ear; the walls fell with a loud discordant crash, and he awoke, hurled from his bed, and stretched, bleeding, on the floor of the cabin. Loud shrieks now reverberated around him; he gained his feet, and with difficulty reached the deck; all was darkness and confusion; he heard a harsh and terrible voice give some indistinct commands, he staggered forward, was lifted from his insecure footing, and stunned at the same instant by a heavy blow: a long period of insensibility transpired, and when he awoke, as from a fearful dream, he was stretched upon a bed; strange forms were around him; strange voices in a foreign tongue addressed him: he collected for an instant his scattered thoughts, and learned, with horror, that the gallant ship in which he had sailed from Liverpool, had been run down in the darkness of the night by a French packet, on her way to Havre, on board of which he now was, being, of all the crew and passengers of the fated Albion, the sole-saved! and sole-survivor!

Leaving Jasper Hamilton on board the stranger ship, where his situation obtained him commiseration and every kind attention, we must retrograde in our story, to relate events which immediately preceded and followed his departure from England.

The health of Sir Edgar Hamilton had been for some time declining, and during the confinement necessary on increasing indisposition, the reflections consequent on anticipated dissolution produced a change in his feelings towards his long estranged son. He thought of the last injunctions of her who had been the idol of his young affections, and the companion of his happiest years, and his heart relented to her fondly cherished offspring. His inquiries were now continually for Jasper; why came he not to receive his parting blessing and forgiveness?—he knew that he lived, and, like the patriarch of old, he yearned to see him before he died. His anxiety was hourly increased by the information given him by his elder-born—that all efforts to discover the location of his brother had been ineffectual; he had left his residence, he said suddenly, without notice given even to him who had been, on all occasions, his friend and advocate; and the confiding father believed his story, and little deemed that the pale and anxious watcher of his uneasy slumbers was, in fact, himself the unworthy cause of all his waking anguish.

Gerard Hamilton, the elder son of Sir Edgar, had long considered that the time might arrive when his father's anger towards his brother would be either entirely obliterated, or, at least, so partially removed, as to interfere with his base and greedy hopes; and he had rendered him pecuniary assistance to prevent the necessity of his making any further application to his father, which he feared, by chance, might reach Sir Edgar, and frustrate his plans of aggrandizement;—this measure, with the inutility and utter hopelessness of such applications, which he had strongly impressed upon Jasper, produced the effect desired; and he had, for a length of time, abandoned their repetition.

The alarming illness and change in his father's frame of mind had, however, suddenly aroused the fears of the wily Gerard; and hence the brilliant prospects held out to his depressed and unhappy brother, and which had induced his immediate departure. He had kept his word, however, as far as regarded the protection of his wife, whom he had placed in an elegant and comfortable seclusion, far removed from the metropolis. Assured in his own mind that the period of Jasper's return was indefinite, and trusting that long before that period could possibly arrive his hopes would be matured by the demise of his father, he resolved to keep him still in ignorance of the real cause of his brother's absence, which would have been a sufficient excuse for the apparent neglect on his part, and might have produced effects favourable to his interests; and he even hinted, with dark malignity, that the well-known stubbornness of his temper, most probably, on this occasion, rendered it voluntary.

Such was the position of affairs on the evening of the day Sir Edgar Hamilton was not expected to survive, precisely five weeks from Jasper's departure.

"No tidings of your brother?" feebly ejaculated the fast-sinking Baronet, raising his head with difficulty towards Gerard, who, at that moment, entered the room, and approached his side. He shook his head, and whispered some vague and indistinct hope that he might yet arrive; for it had been all along the policy of Gerard to sustain, by such surmises, the lingering expectations of his anxious parent, who now sunk exhausted on his pillow.

He arose, and quietly paced the apartment; a few hours, and his expectations would be realized; his brother was on the wide sea, far removed from all chance of reconciliation with his father, whose existence a few short hours would terminate; when the title, the broad lands, and *all* the accumulated wealth of years would be his own. From these pleasing meditations he was aroused by the voice of his father:—" Where is Jasper ?" wildly exclaimed the delirious and dying man; " Why comes he not? Is he sent for?" Gerard hastened to his side, and endeavoured to calm and soothe him; the medical attendants were called, but he still continued to rave of Jasper.

" He will be here," cried Gerard; " I have again sent to seek him; he will most surely come, dear father."

At this instant a carriage, the rattling sound of its rapid motion partly muffled by the arrangements of the street, might be distinctly heard to stop before the door of the mansion ;—a bustle was heard in the hall, and then the hasty steps of a man upon the stairs. " It is my boy," exclaimed Sir Edgar, " I know his footstep; he comes at last to bless me !" Gerard gazed an instant with an expression of blended doubt and alarm, when the door opened, and Jasper Hamilton knelt by the bedside of his father.

With his long lost son returned, for a brief interval, both his strength and reason. " Reach me," he said, " yonder cabinet." He was obeyed; a secret spring opened a drawer; and with a firm hand he drew forth a sealed paper. " A lighted taper," he cried, " quick ;" it was brought; " witness all," he said, " my last act and deed ;—thus I destroy the document which *disinherited my son*." The bright flame fed fiercely on the fatal instrument, and, as its last portion shrivelled beneath its influence, a faint smile lighted, for a moment, the features of the dying man, and, with his eye fixed to the last on Jasper, without a sigh he expired.

Having seen quite sufficient in the slave state of Maryland to sicken me with the idea of American liberty, I retraced my steps, and one very fine morning embarked at New York and arrived safely at Liverpool, determined to give my fellow countrymen the benefit of my observations ; and more than ever satisfied that there is more *genuine* liberty in England than in any of the Thirteen States of the

Highly-vaunted Republic !

F I N I S.

www.ingramcontent.com/pod-product-compliance
Lightning Source LLC
Chambersburg PA
CBHW081213170626
46811CB00010B/3273